Grove grew up in New Hampshire with a family of five and a love of reading as a way of exploring new worlds. It wasn't until a profound meeting with loss and grief that her writing took form, and her first novel was completed. Now she lives in Colorado, with her spouse and small family of animals, with hopes of new stories to tell.

To Mom, for better or worse, you are dearly missed.

H.E. Grove

INTO THE WILD BLUE

AUSTIN MACAULEY PUBLISHERS™

LONDON • CAMBRIDGE • NEW YORK • SHARJAH

Ordering Information
Quantity sales: Special discounts are available on quantity purchases by corporations, associations, and others. For details, contact the publisher at the address below.

Publisher's Cataloging-in-Publication data
Grove, H.E.
Into the Wild Blue

ISBN 9798889107866 (Paperback)
ISBN 9798889107873 (ePub e-book)

Library of Congress Control Number: 2023924636

www.austinmacauley.com/us

First Published 2024
Austin Macauley Publishers LLC
40 Wall Street, 33rd Floor, Suite 3302
New York, NY 10005
USA

mail-usa@austinmacauley.com
+1 (646) 5125767

To Dad, Isabeau, Mckenna, and Dante, any good that has happened thus far has been because of you.

Table of Contents

Green

Green is a color most odd; it mixes and merges with other hues to create its own cycle. Green is the harbinger of change along with the nature of life itself in all of its forms.

Mountain ranges are the perfect representation of this phenomenon. When bathed in the golden rays of afternoon sun, they roll forward swaddled in a lush green quilt freckled with patches of white and blue wildflowers. The leaves of the trees act as a filter to tint the yellow drips of the sun into a transparent green and dapple the ground of their gem-like refractions. At one point to inspire the creation of poems and songs to its majesty, another to beckon explorers to observe life in its prime element of creation. Such is the glory of midday, with the sun at his peak and the world basking in his light.

Dusk yields a more dreary, soulful blue green to bring tidings of the dark hours approaching. When it becomes the time for little ones to be tucked safely away from the creeping blue to black. It's during these times that the forms of flora and fauna blur, swirl together, or even switch places entirely. Creatures forgotten by time and preserved only by myth stir and rise to stumble among the jagged peaks and sloping valleys. The moon replaces her glorious cousin in the sky and casts her darkling aura over all things; transmogrifying them into their most primal states.

All meanings of fantastical and unnatural things happen when the sun goes down. Human history depicted these times often transcending what is natural and good and giving way to chaos. Advised by such tales of danger and woe, man has since cowered from the shadowy magic that stains everything around into unnatural shapes and colors. Then again one must ponder that, in the absence of laws to define what order is, whether the line between natural and unnatural exists at all.

The Haven

For all its ever-changing forms and hues, the ripples of skyward rock always felt like a sanctuary to our weary Traveler, a quiet man content enough passing his remaining years listening to the howling mountaintop gales and drinking from icy stream waters. Decades of walking under the sun and through harsh wind had etched lines into his face that exaggerated the presence of his stern expression. He lived a lonely existence save for a few clucking hens in a broken-down cottage tucked into a safe thicket of short evergreens. Perched safely on top of a mountain surrounded by peaks on all sides. Its walls stood firm against the wind blowing in from the tundra that coated the land, but the inhabitant would be left shivering in its wake.

Despite all that, it was comfortable enough inside with the smell of all the things from the earth. Bundles of herbs hung neatly on clean walls, emitting a soft floral aroma. Little pots of soil harbored precious little plants that wouldn't last a day in the frozen soil outside. They yielded tomatoes and peppers in the summer, and quiet companionship for the rest of the year. Not much in that hovel preached anything other than necessity, except for a single fox pelt on the wood floor, and even that served a purpose.

During the chillier winter mornings, the old man liked the cushion of the soft fur on his sore feet. A pleasant difference from the hardwood flooring inside the hut. There were two windows that gave morning and dusk colors permission to tint the peeling paint. On fairer days, they let a delicious spring wind air out the incumbent mustiness of the house.

This morning, the stranger awoke to a mural of golden and red dancing on the ceiling above his head, and the first warm breeze of the coming summer ruffling his silvery hair. He relished the summer and all her gifts; getting older made him enjoy the ease and plenty of the season that much more. *Such a lovely morning was owed its own celebration*, he thought to himself.

Climbing out of the warm pile of furs and textiles that served as his bed had only gotten harder with age. The slightest bit of cold seeped into his bones and joints more and more each passing year. He quickly, but clumsily, changed into the simple linen and knitted clothes that kept the mountain chills away. His knuckles grew sore and swollen from years of worsening arthritis. Nonetheless, he began his day with a determined vigor.

Before the more enjoyable part of the morning, he had a list of chores that came with the rising sun. The small red hens were clamoring to be let out of the small coop to peck at each other in the yard and await their supper. They were impatient to go about their lazy day. Their caretaker stooped his back with a groan and peered into each nest on the off chance of seeing any surprises. To his good luck, he was rewarded with not one, but two smooth brown eggs.

They were still warm; his rough fingers ran over the hard surface of the shells, feeling the tiny bumps that interrupted the smoothness. The unexpectedness of such a treat pulled a crooked smile from the old man as he slipped them into the pocket of his rough burlap apron. The garden of pots was ripe with a few tomatoes and even a bright, yellow pepper. If he waited a bit longer, he could have a robust red pepper rather than the sweeter gold.

Patience gave way to excitement, and he twisted the vegetable off its stem with a soft snap. The tomatoes were firm but gave way when he pressed a little harder on them. He was pleased, they wouldn't disintegrate into mush when he sliced them. Slipping these little gems of nature into another pocket, the Traveler set about preparing his meal.

This came in the form of poached eggs on top of a coarse brown bread paired with his favorite tea, a sweet drink brewed with blue flowers from the side of a mountain a few miles away. Those beautiful vegetables were to be placed directly on the flames to form a delicious char, and then sliced thinly and placed on top of the slabs of bread. The eggs went last, crowning the breakfast in a coronal of rich gold. Despite being a wholesome meal, most of the pleasure came not from the consumption but rather the preparation. The mix of different steams and the sounds of cooking warmed both the home and the cook.

Everything from the soft rolling boil of water in a pot to the spitting sizzle of roasting vegetables. Now rendered limp and glossy, the brightly colored pepper slid perfectly into place on top of the toasted bread. He topped it all with the smoothly poached eggs with their orange yolks coated in a milky membrane and a dash of precious salt. For this occasion, he even snipped off a leaf of his young mint plant to swirl about in his tea to add an awakening freshness, a nice change from everything being dried. After all of it, he stood back and gazed with pride at his creation; the colors of the food he prepared now mirrored the lights dancing around his ceiling as the day began his wake.

A small table by the east-facing window provided some scenery with breakfast. It overlooked beyond the edge of the young trees to reveal the caps and hills of the surrounding landscape. The sun hovered just about a heavy grey curtain as the morning moisture lingered in the air below the summit. Only the very peaks poked through it in a mossy green and sharp black rock. The old man enjoyed his early mornings like this; watching the earth still sleepy and blanketed by the low-bearing sky. The chill in the air before the summer sun could warm the roof of the world balanced perfectly with the steamy food to warm his insides. Slowly eating, to better relish the flavors and perhaps extend the pleasant moment, the Traveler watched this same wispy blanket recede into the valleys below. The jaggedness of the earth revealed its characteristic unwavering strength. With his many summers of refuge here, he had come to know these peaks very well.

At his first arrival at the top of the world, he had thought himself a man already, but now looking back, he was barely out of childhood. It happened eons ago, when the sun had finally set on the dominion of man. Back then he had some companions, his grandparents, and the few other vagabonds and nomads one encounters over countless miles of journey.

He came with them on an exodus toward some unknown end. He didn't know much other than that they kept telling him each night, that they were going home. Which puzzled his then childish mind to no end as he thought they had already left home. What other home were they walking to? His grandparents were resolute in this and pushed onward through a creeping wilderness that grew with each new moon. They were always lovers of nature and knew more than most about the unlikely refuge that the forest of peaks and valleys offered.

It was their steady guidance that brought a child from the cradle of civilization into a man just as wily and wild as the surrounding terrain. His instincts were sharpened by years of peril and isolation from others. Yet, sometimes, if he let his thoughts wander too far from the present moment, he wondered if they were proud of the life he led. There lingered in his ears when everything was quiet, the expectation of something more.

The memories of them and their expectations of him were fading into obscurity with the encroaching infirmities of an aging mind. The gentle clamor of their voices lost to the ravages of time and their silhouettes broken up against the horizon. All that was left of them now was the wind and sky and perhaps the Traveler himself, as the culmination of all their efforts.

Despite the staggering solitude that surrounded the Traveler, there seemed to be no cause for him to fall into despair. For all intents and purposes, he led a good life. He rarely went to sleep hungry and the simple cottage provided a kinder home than many he had seen on his travels. Coming across it as a younger man, it was nothing more than four walls holding rubble. He used his own two hands to rebuild and patch the roof using wood and clay from the river in the valley below.

Using yet more clay and stones, he fixed its fireplace and chimney back into working order. Back then he must have been in his early twenties, so he was able to hurry about this work before the wind became bitter. After he was sure that his handiwork would withstand the piles of snow, it would expect in the winter; he was content to finally move into its sanctuary. Over time, its threshold filled with plants and items to give evidence of his existence within its walls. He tamed some feral chickens that he had found lurking around the surrounding woods and made them a modest home to guard them from foxes or wolves.

Not that many bothered him anyway. Either out of ignorance of what he was or simply fear; animals steered clear of him when they sensed his approach. On that mountaintop, he made his home; safe, sheltered, and satisfied, he wanted for nothing that he needed. He was prepared to live out the rest of his days picking vegetables and foraging roots for the winters when he could curl up by his neat little fire and sleep the cold away.

And he had done just that for an eternity; that being said, there was a void hanging in the center of his existence. Not unlike a heavy stone that, when swallowed, weighs deeply and heavily in one's belly. Somewhere in his decades of wandering he had left something behind.

Long ago maybe, there was a word that poets, songbirds, and romantics alike used for it. The exact term eluded the old man. He recalled the one book that had stayed with him through his travels; it was currently wedged under a short leg of his breakfast table to level it. Somewhere in its withering pages was such a word and its application.

It was attributed to the lack of something that was once present. The term insinuated a new mystery in of itself because there was no hint as to where to look. The lonely old man no longer had use for such words as there was no one to speak him to who wasn't covered in feathers or pine needles. He spent hours of his time pushing such thoughts stubbornly from his mind and convincing himself that he was content with the life that fate had gifted him.

Still, it persisted like waves of nausea. A feeling in his gut that his body had to expel through the mouth. He ignored the discomfort and went about his slow eating, insisting inwardly that the taste of his food wasn't fading into mush. So adamant was he that all was well everything was in its proper place.

But indeed, there used to be something there, in between the lungs and perched on top of the stomach. Perhaps among the vast lands he traveled, it had been mislaid, displaced. Our lonely stranger must have left it somewhere and forgotten about it. Perhaps he ate it during a particularly hard winter years ago that had buried the cottage in snow and thick sheets of ice. Leaving to sour in his stomach and try to climb out years later. He felt the word tumble through his throat and through his lips to meet with the cold world outside. "Lost."

The word was short, surprisingly so; there was almost a beauty to it. However, his voice, raspy and quiet from disuse, seemed to drag it out and give it claws to rake the air with its sound. The simplicity of the word reverberated through the gentle sounds of nature with its surprising harshness. Something about the pronunciation of the consonants at the end of it bit into his tongue with a sharp edge.

That edge cut him deep within himself. It sliced its way through flesh and bone into the windy chasm of his chest to carve its spelling into the emptiness. In remembering that term, he recalled in painful detail its application.

The egg had gone cold at this point and lay there sad and hardened on top of the chipped plate. Such a shame for this delicacy to go to waste. So the old man ate it with the same languid energy that was used for all menial tasks. After his meal was gone, the old man sat there a long time as if he was suddenly and rudely roused from a dream to which he was desperately trying to return. He didn't get up to resume his day until the air was warmed enough by an early afternoon sun, so deep was his reverie.

His day carried on with this new burden eating away at him, nonetheless. A listless nature hovered over him as he tended to his home. There was a pinprick-sized hole in the far corner of his cottage, furthest from his bed. It let in a chill at night that compromised his safe box of warm air. To patch it he harvested some sticky tree sap from the nearby trees and, very carefully as to not smear the stuff on his skin, plugged the leak. He didn't mind being very dirty, but sap was especially stubborn and difficult to scrub loose.

It was while the Traveler was toting a bounty of forage from the nearby valley that the air suddenly shifted to come from a different direction. It carried a new scent, a salty tinge. The breeze had brought with it the smell of the Traveler's seaside origin. It had been years; might as well have been a while lifetime since he had anything to remind him of home. *How curious*, he thought to himself, that the same day he realized what he had lost was the day that an unlikely gift was now blowing across the tundra.

He breathed deep, and let the salt take him back in time to a little village by a massive gray ocean. Like this sea itself, his memories overflowed, and he was plunged chokingly into the depths of nostalgia. The acrid sensation was entering into his nostrils and filling his brain with things he'd long since forgotten. In his long life, he had seen so much taken from him with reckless abandon. He now remembered a house on the edge of a cliff that overlooked the dark water.

A sharp, herbal smell wafting from clouds of purple and white cloth brushing softly along his cheek. He remembered a hot, bitter liquid mixing melodiously with chilly mornings. The sad comfort of this flooded the lungs of the Traveler; it coursed through his veins like a river and spilled waterfalls from his eyes. His hot tears turned cold in the incoming wind and stung his skin as they trickled down his withered cheeks. In that moment, the Traveler felt, as if for the first time, truly alone.

The Horizon

Before the Traveler arrived at the place where earthen rock pierces sky, there had been a very long journey. It began in what seemed like another time. Perhaps it did. He never forgot who it was that guided him to his present home, nor the role they played in his long survival. However, it was now that he remembered, in painful clarity, the joy they showed him during his childish years.

For a blissful time, he had his grandparents to share in the daily delights of poached eggs on toast and fill the silence with laughter and light-hearted conversation. Hardship had not yet worn down their smiles and stolen away their health. It was their hands, in unison, that guided his fledgling footsteps forward. When danger loomed overhead, it was them who spirited him away across the land in hopes of reaching some place they spoke of few times and named even less. They would never make it to the end of their exodus.

A fate met them that had come for all of humanity eventually. One day they were with him, teaching him the ways of the world, the next they had vanished. Their existence scattered to the harsh winds of the wilderness. All that remained of them now were memories trapped in the brain of a silent old man running out of time of his own. The memories of that adventure they shared faded considerably in a wash of time and neglect.

For when one forgets to tend to the fragile pictures hung delicately in the mind, they become entombed in immovable dust, and the images are lost. That didn't stop him from grasping at them desperately now, to regain that clarity. The scent coming in from the west and blowing over the rolling hills and sharply edged cliffs was beckoning him to seek it out and reclaim what was indeed lost.

In spite of recent epiphanies, the old man stood resolute in his pragmatic ways. He thought himself too advanced in age to undertake such a task. He found himself inwardly debating this for three days; all while being pelted day in and day out by this summons from the distant horizon. It was almost as if it had a tireless need to announce its presence, and thus nagged him relentlessly through any wall, blanket, or wrapping with its icy salt. No amount of sleep or warm, flowered tea took the thoughts blowing in from the dark hills.

For all intents and purposes, he was content to stay there for the decade or so he had left in this tall, harsh world. He fought that temptation back with his almost unwavering practicality. He was too old for adventures, had already made his bed, and determined to lie in it. When he was small enough to barely reach his grandfather's knee, he would tell himself that one day he would be an explorer, a traveler of many paths. This childish fantasy soon evaporated, funny enough, when his wish was granted, and he found himself on the run from everything known.

The rough journey ahead had given him a bitterness toward such an idea, but now he looked back on those days with a dry humor at the irony of it all. Eventually, he succumbed to the need to be a wanderer once more and acknowledged his calling. He had been told, one day at the very beginning, their destination by his grandparents. Since then, their path had skewed and veered so much off course that he wasn't sure if even they remembered where they were going. What he did remember were blurry vignettes of the journey up to this point and the direction toward each. Simple landmarks.

The distance had taken them years to cross, and there was a very good reason for leaving. He wasn't the energetic youth he once was, and the likelihood of his untimely end was front and center of his thoughts. Though death was too close and too imminent for him to properly fear it, he had no desire to go out painfully. Such a large risk to just go backward. That being said, the salty air commanded, and the old man was compelled to obey.

The sun was blocked by thick, gray clouds when the final decision was made. Packing for such a journey was simple; plentiful lands lay between the beginning and the end of the path ahead. The Traveler, as he would now call himself in his own mind, took an inventory of the wall of herbs and medicines he had painstakingly preserved over the years. He knew he couldn't take all of them. As age crept slowly over his bones, he woke each morning with a new ache or bruise.

Sickness fell on him quicker and more brutally than in previous years. He found comfort in the many gifts that the earth gave him through its flora. The most important of these were blackberry leaves; he brewed their leaves with honeysuckle into a tea to relieve the joint pain that had become his frequent visitor. After that went in, Horsemint and Cinchona bark for possible fevers and injuries that would occur along the way. All of these were put into woven bags and placed carefully at the foot of his bed.

The rest would have to stay behind to turn to dust along with anything else left there. However, much to the bemusement of the Traveler, there would always be room for extra salt and dried blue flower petals. Such delicacies were too rare and too good to pass up. Among the more sensible items were an extra set of clothing, a thick, waxy canvas, and his beautiful bone knife. From a dusty wooden box beneath the bed, our nomad brought out a weathered canvas bag with more patches than pockets and a pair of leather boots that he had never bothered to wear since his grandfather did.

However, he put them on now to find that they were a near perfect fit and likely a much better choice for footwear than his leather moccasins. He took a step back with a resounding thud as the hard sole hit the floor and looked long at the items he planned to take along with him. After a while, he nodded to himself with satisfaction and began to tuck each article into it with an almost military neatness.

Packing for the journey was only half of the process that the old man set himself to in order to prepare for his departure. He felt obligated to care for the lives he spent his years to nurturing. He planted the younger vegetable plants beside their older neighbors outside in the garden to catch the raindrops and hopefully flourish. Even if he was not here to harvest, they could, at the very least, feed the wildlife that would retake the cottage. There was one matter of business that left a cold knot in the pit of the man's stomach.

Over the years in that thicket, he had formed a gentle fondness toward the chickens that he housed in the coop. During the years he had cared for their every need and been their keeper, they grew into fat and lazy birds. Many a night he came to the rescue of their horrified crows to chase away some fox or wildcat away from their shelter. Without him, they wouldn't last a full month before the predators of the area realized their vulnerability. He trudged over to their pen and peered down at them pecking at the ground and each other in unburdened business.

Shutting them in the coop and letting starvation pick them off felt unnecessarily cruel. Not even a way he himself wanted to die. Slaughtering each hen and burying the carcasses had no use to anything but the maggots and the carrion birds. That also eliminated any chance of them actually somehow surviving without their guardian. They were only birds, but they had provided the Traveler with companionship and sustenance over the years. And that indebted him to them. No matter how little their knowledge of it was.

He wrestled with this conundrum as he tarried about preparing the cottage for its pending emptiness. He knew there were no more humans left to discover this safe haven, but much like the chickens, he felt indebted to the respite it had given him over the years. He boarded up the windows and folded the furs he was leaving behind into neat bundles on the mattress stuffed with dried grass. He was putting away the items in the kitchen when the realization struck him; he hadn't planned on taking any cookware.

He had a small cast iron pan that his grandmother had found before they crossed the great plains. It was heavy for its size, but the Traveler's hands seemed unable to put it down. He stood there feeling the cool, rough metal against his skin and attached it to the pack with a leather cord. With it, he tied a ceramic pot he would use for teas and soup when it was cold outside.

That night he ate his last meal in the kind shelter of the lonely cottage. The food weighed heavily on his tongue. The bed felt that much more comfortable with many nights of sleeping on the ground ahead of him. That night, the crickets chirped happily through the especially warm air and a soft whistle echoed in the distant trees.

It was like the whole mountaintop knew of his coming departure the next morning and was singing him a farewell song. He slept soundly and woke just as the sun was peeking his bright yellow face through a pink sky. It was time for him to go.

The Walk

The journey began with heavy boot steps leading away from an empty cottage, awaiting another lost soul that would never arrive. The neat stores of medicine and furs that much colder for being alone once more. The door to the coop swaying openly in the morning air with the sheltered fowls shifting in their nests and clucking nervously among themselves. Within himself, he hoped that they would survive to go back to the wild nature he had found them in.

Their protector was gone now, and their shelter disabled; it felt heartless to do such a thing to such weak animals. Their only hope was to hustle down the slopes to the warmer valleys to survive the winter. The tundra at the top of the world had no place for weak creatures. But their existence had to serve a purpose; they would either live among other birds and flourish, or they would perish and feed the strong. What other purpose did they have to begin with?

There wasn't a specific path that the old man remembered would bring him back to the sea. His only certainty was that he needed to cross the wide-open plains beyond the mountain range. After that, he knew of a few landmarks that could point him closer to home. Those lay west of him, so at least there was a start. He didn't dare to look back as he walked, the journey beginning with a descent down the mountainside.

The ground was covered in soft grass and red clover blossoms and a gentle breeze rustled the treetops. Once the old man reached a low enough altitude, the trees changed from spiky evergreens into light green aspens with their crisp white trunks and other broadleaf trees. This was the best time of year to see all of nature in full bloom. The angle of the hill, however, had painful consequences for his old bones.

His knees groaned at him for the effort and sometimes when he took an especially steep descent, he heard a crackle as his body adapted to the new movement. It would only take him an hour to arrive in the valley that lay at the foot of his mountain. He was familiar with the area; he often descended the mountain to trap and forage. Just as he knew the area, it seemed to know him as well.

He passed by a lynx lapping absentmindedly at a creek cutting through the wood. He had been curious about this of course, but over the years had become grateful for one less problem. And he already had the elements of the changing seasons to weather through. He steadily trudged onward toward his last familiar stop. A remote, abandoned village tucked into the trees, not unlike his own cottage.

Sometimes, when he needed something the land could not offer, he would make brief excursions into the desecrated buildings. Figured it would be alright if he spent the last night for a while within sturdy four walls before he set out on the final walk. The town was small, with only four buildings picked clean by the Traveler for his various errands. Nature had overtaken it long ago and covered the barren planks and poles in a blanket of lush green vines.

Him being a quiet soul and appreciative of the earth, smaller birds and prey mammals weren't shy toward his presence as a result. On many foraging trips, he would pause to feed a herd of deer wandering through with their fawns or engage in prolonged eye contact with a rabbit worriedly huddled in tall grasses. He enjoyed these times, the subtle twitching of the soft muzzles against his palms and the way the fine white eyelashes over their big eyes were pleasing. A gentleness emanated from these creatures in such a way that cleansed the world around them.

Today was different, however, the forest had an eerie silence weaving in between the trunks of the trees. There were animals, but they stood at attention, still as a rock. Even the fawns that dared never leave their mother's side stood stiffly with their oversized ears pricked. The wanderer knew why; there may have been a time when such phenomena were considered otherworldly. Anyone who would bother drawing such useless conclusions was no more, so such events were now as mundane and happenstance as a full moon or a chilly gust of wind.

So many years ago, seemingly before the stranger could recall clearly, he heard adult voices speaking in hushed tones of Old Gods rising from forgotten graves. He spent the majority of his boyhood believing this to be a myth or one of those strange parts of grownup conversations where they use one thing to mean another. The child grew into the strength of adulthood brushing away such stories like dust on his shoulder. None such creatures had crossed his path and his infinitely practical mind predicted that would continue. That being said, one hot summer day, the day that he ventured into the rocky cradle of the world.

Before him appeared a graven image; so immense was its strangeness. The then-young eyes of the Traveler not quite comprehending what was before them. That was the first and only time that he had seen the thing. However, he had learned over the years the different omens of its approach. It began as a gentle rumble; something of enormous size was sweeping across the valleys and hills toward the old man.

An uneasiness gnawed the lining of his stomach; he had no desire to see it again. He continued with a heightened urgency quickening his pace, praying inwardly to no one that he was small enough to be shielded from sight by the trees and underbrush. The creature was close now, closing the distance with each thunderous step. He could see a nearby pond ripple on its surface from the impact on the soft ground. Thus far, he had nothing to fear from it, but there is always the fear of the unknown, or all that is too wild and beyond the possible control of man.

He sensed it drawing ever closer and took shelter behind an old, dead oak tree; its trunk holding the girth that came with centuries of growth. After a short while, the eldritch thing's long, spindly legs appeared walking carefully through the trees. Merely looking skyward enlightened the old man on what truly fed the nightmares of the last humans.

Its appearance brought to life the nighttime blend of plant and beast. Its hulking torso a bundle of roots and ribs flowing together in a geometry that was either divine or accursed. Truly like a giant that slumbered so long that flora had begun to take root in its sleeping form. The entire being was shaped like a titanic stag propped up on its hind legs. It towered above the treetops, surveying its dominion through eyeless sockets.

A whistle sang from its mouth high above the treetops, a melodious, shrill sound. Not quite elk, nor was it a wolf howl either. The living god seemed to not walk but glide over its reclaimed domain with graceful strides. The enormous claws at the end of its long arms brushed aside the trees as if they were nothing but bushes in its path. Taking great care not to rip branches from their trunks or displace the small creek making its way through the valley.

The old man felt his legs shaking at the sight of it, the devolved majesty of the thing. This was the creature that shared its kingdom with him; its distinctive howl echoed across the rolling hills and cliffs often when the moon was dark and the air had a chill to it. Something about autumn made the thing uneasy, he remembered. He wondered briefly if it was the cold or the apprehension of the coming winter that it disliked.

He remained painfully still while the thing passed him by; his sore, arthritic joints screaming at him to move even an inch. Only when he was sure of the safe distance between them did he dare walk across the wake that it left despite its best efforts to leave the land untouched. There was no avoiding the craters its monumental hooves left in the soft earth.

How ironic it seemed to the Traveler how the call to adventure often led one through weeks of the same surroundings. The supposed monotony he was walking through began each day, as a cycle of rising with the sun to a breakfast of odds and ends. Usually, the dried meats he carried with him and some assorted wild vegetables he found along the way. He would leisurely trek through the trees and flowering fields until the sun went down, and then dinner while witnessing the last bits of peach and red sky be overtaken by the deepest indigo.

Over the course of his life, he had heard poems and songs about the beauty and romanticism of the stars in the night sky. But to his eyes, they were staring uncomfortably at him in a hard, cold glare. The sheer number of them felt invasive to his peaceful solitude. He discovered that he didn't enjoy the feeling of being looked at, being observed.

The old man didn't hate it, the years he spent alone in the wilds of the mountains. He had become accustomed to the eternal cycle of the elements. The migration of green to gold to white in the earth and the endless blues of the sky. Within the workings of the world, the Traveler found little moments of bliss. He enjoyed the occasional rainfall that created music as the drops of water bounced merrily off the leaves to land on the soft ground.

A few days later, delicate stems of green would shoot bravely upward toward the sun. After a few decades of this close observation, the old man found that he could sometimes detect the breed of plant at its very first leaf. He thought it to be some sort of game that he could place bets on; his competitor was the earth itself. *Green was his favorite color*, he thought, *because of the precious life that clung to it.*

Even among the reds and yellows and pinks that blossomed in the earth and sky couldn't compare to its simplicity. It was for this reason that the old man stopped to gaze for a while at the tiny sprout, pondering its courage to bloom in that lively green among the brown dirt and gray rocks.

In this slow, careful manner, hours passed in a blissful silence broken only by the chirps of a distant lark and the snapping of small twigs underfoot. The Traveler always took care to tread lightly wherever he stepped, to avoid breaking that spell. Every so often the shrill cry of the behemoth in the distance pierced the reverie. The trees and fresh green leaves shuddered with each piercing howl. The animals he came across were unbothered by the sound; a herd of deer just continued their leisurely graze whenever it sounded, but flinched away from his own footsteps drawing near.

He was puzzled at its travel pattern; the two wanderers crossed paths more often than what the old man was comfortable with. Having the sense to take cover whenever he felt those thundering footsteps didn't stop curiosity from needling its way through his skull. He hadn't dared crane his neck to peer at its face, usually shrouded by the canopy of the forest. One of these times, when the two met in a beetle-eaten section of trees where their branches stood barren against the sky, he took a wild chance. He couldn't take it anymore and peeked around the trunk of the maple shielding his presence. What he saw froze his blood and turned his very bones to stone.

From its skull, misshapen branches sprouted leaves that melted into yellow feathers. The creature was looking at him, he was faced with the direct glare of its eyeless gaze. The pearly bone of its toothless jaw was adorned with moss and vines that only emphasized the emptiness where there should've been pupils and irises. It hadn't stopped its patrol but kept its slow stalking through the woods. Nonetheless, it knew of the old human trekking through its territory.

And it wanted him to know that. The whole exchange took no longer than a couple of seconds, but to the one dwarfed by the other, it might as well have been hours. When his mastery of his limbs was returned to him from the shackles of fright, he ducked quickly back behind the tree and crawled to the safety of some thick bushes. Adrenaline flooded his veins, and he listened rabidly to the footsteps leading away from him. His ears pulsed with fear until he was certain that the threat had gone away and then all his strength left him.

The moments that immediately follow panic are the most terrifying of all; it's when your body relinquishes the instinct to survive and gives way to exhaustion. Your limbs grow heavy, and for a brief moment, you think that your heart has stopped beating. The shock catches up with you, and you are reminded by your own body just how weak and vulnerable you are. This cold feeling took over the Traveler and brought him crashing to his knees, panting.

His lungs desperately tried to take air in and bring his blood back to life as the corners of his vision tinged purple and blue. At the base of the maple tree, he was stranded by this comedown of weariness. Eventually, he could feel the energy slowly returning, and he could stand. He had been warned, put in his place by the true king of these mountains. And it was with that new burden that he was saddled with, that he continued to walk west.

As his journey went on, the days passed into weeks until the deep, lush greens of summer turned golden and bronze. The forest colors became warmer in direct contrast to the new bitterness of the air. The only things unchanged were the tall evergreens remaining astutely green with their spires of fragrant needles. Our companion found this time of year to be the most dazzling and exciting, albeit the most unsure. The swirling golds, reds, and lingering bits and green preached joy and beckoned one to sit and watch their intricate dance.

But years of survival had taught his old bones to brace for the hardship that followed this beauty. Not soon after the small palettes of color withered off their branches would the cruel, hungry winter come. All the small prey animals would scurry into the safety of their warm burrows to slumber the cold and danger away. His season of plenty would end, and having left shelter behind months ago, the Traveler had a long way to go before sanctuary.

The Camp

As the days continued to shorten and the moon rose with the setting sun, the Traveler took a brief hiatus from his walking for meager preparation for the coming season. A clearing he saw that surrounded a small, clear lake seemed like a good enough spot to rest. By that time, the leaves had begun to fall and the ground was painted with a mural of crunchy yellow and red colors already turning brown. There was a peace here that flushed new strength back into the old man. It was only for a few weeks to stock up provisions and then set off to travel through the winter.

On the shore of the lake, he assembled a modest hut with young trees all cut and trimmed to surround the trunk of a towering oak. Its sturdiness was unlikely to topple from the wind and the saplings would provide excellent structure; he draped his tent canvas over the branches to create the final seal against fall rain. Having coated it with a fine layer of wax, it was waterproof and bound to keep him dry. Without a boat, the Traveler could only fish along the shallows for smaller trout, but even they were enough. He allowed himself to waste a few hours along the water's edge to catch his dinner and indulge in the freshness of the season.

Onto the harder part of the project, the Traveler set about digging a considerably large hole in the ground a few hundred paces away from the shelter. In it, he threw discarded wood pieces and carefully selected stones from the shoreline. Using leftover saplings to create a small roof over this hole, the Traveler took some wire from his pack and strung it across what would be smoldering embers. The smoking hut would dry out and preserve any food he would get a hold of and make it carriable.

That, and he loved the flavor it infused into meats. Staying at the top of a mountain had made smoked fish an especially rare treat, so this alone was a cause for a crooked tug at the corners of his old mouth. That night, the warm, salty flesh of that day's catch filled our companion's belly. The night blurred into a slump of satisfied drowsiness and sleep came cloaked in the dark autumn sky.

Dreams came softly at first to the slumbering mind of the weary old Traveler. The time of day was always the same in the Traveler's dreams, the murky lilac gray of dusk. This curious afterglow permeated through the soft linen coverings of a window. A lacy, white hem brushed his cheek gently. There was a smell in the soft air beside the salt of the nearby sea.

It was bitter and nutty, an aftertaste of citrus and an accompanying draft of sharp lavender. He knew the scent. Coffee it was called, the taste was best paired with the morning sun and the sweet abandon of bed. An extinct taste, but you only have to have it a few times to commit it to memory; the elixir seeped in to erase fatigue and left traces of that bitterness. His grandmother loved coffee; the dream reminded him of her always having a mug full of it.

The scent of the dark beverage brought back a vision of her laugh-lined face that spoke of her good nature before her mouth even opened. That scent again, the spicy bite of fresh lavender. Her perfume filled his nostrils as the dreamer felt the brush of skin as warm fingers tucked hair from his temple. Her long nails gently scratched his scalp in a surprisingly soothing sensation. His skin was softer back then, less lined, and defined by years of struggle.

Her soft, husky voice murmured things that weren't quite words in his hazy recollection. The dreamer felt his pulse quicken in excitement over words he couldn't understand. What for? The memory blurred at the source of excitement, and her meaning was unclear. The dream ended with his small body being scooped up into strong arms and the dreamer fell into the deepest state of sleep. Where nothing ever happened, and everything was dark and unmoving.

The Traveler woke to that same dusk monotone in the morning. It was still fairly dark outside the shelter, but the old man pushed his blanket aside and crawled outside to meet the day. Only eager busybodies outrun the sun. But being one such person, our Traveler set about his chores for the day. More fishing rendered a few more small rewards which were hung in the smokehouse.

Branches of firs were piled on top of the roof of the hut to keep the heat in and the cold out. He learned on his first night there exactly where the wind was seeping through the gaps. After these tasks had reached the old man's standards, he ventured off into the surrounding forest to rummage for anything else he could find. Luckily, this forest was bursting at the seams with edible roots and plants. The ground was littered with large, brown acorns that he carefully inspected for worms and then dropped into a specially made bag of netting.

Mushrooms bloomed large and brown on rotting carcasses of fallen trees while their surviving neighbors harbored moss in between their strips of bark. Both gifts from nature went into another empty sack the Traveler carried with him. As the day went on and the bag became heavier; the Traveler found himself blissfully distracted from the troubles of the present. Something about the hard labor drew his concentration. As well as still craning his ears and eyes for possible threats in unfamiliar woodland. A misstep in the wrong place could be as deadly as a snakebite, especially at his age.

His mind drifted to the peaceful rustling of the trees and lazy grazing among the herds of deer as the day went on. The Old God still let out its anguished cry; distance reduced it to a pathetic whisper that had lost its booming influence. Upon returning, the Traveler piled the mushrooms into the smoking hut to lose their moisture and become dry, stiff little morsels for the harder days to come. *A pity*, he thought to himself, *their buttery flavor would wither into a smoky earthiness*. The moss, he took back to the hut and carefully, so as not to tear the delicate things, laid each piece on the cold, hard ground.

Under his sleeping space. Networking the tiny pillows together formed a natural quilt, creating a perfectly suitable patch of cushion for his old bones to lie on. By the time he was finished with his chores, the sky was dimming back to its palette of subdued purple hues. The stars blinked harder from their thrones in the deepening blue, peering down toward the lonely Traveler as he made his dinner and lay upon his mossy bed to dream once again. However, tonight saw no such dream, only a black abyss to absorb any consciousness waiting for the light of day.

This cycle repeated itself many times over the course of weeks; they were spent gathering and fishing. Eating the meat he could get now and preserving what he foraged. He set traps to catch a rabbit or squirrel. The days were spent in pleasant walks through the generous bounty of the woodlands and the nights slept fitfully through until dusky sunrises. The dreams eluded the Traveler's tired mind until the moon hung low and swollen in the inky blackness of the sky.

During its fullness was the only time that dreams visited him. The Traveler often pondered on the nature of this phenomenon, whether it was malevolent or simply one of the mysterious coincidences that occur whenever the shadows grew. He found that night often brought with it all manners of curiosities, especially since the way of man ended long ago and the old, forgotten things that hibernated in the earth emerged. Though memory proved fallible with time, the Traveler could somewhat recall the omen of a bright, looming behemoth before the journey began. It was like the moon, but more yellow and much brighter.

Not unlike the sun, but colder. The old man had faint memories of cowering in fear from it, or what it meant, the details were fuzzy. Throughout the years, the Traveler had come to have a wariness when it came to the nights when the white moon gave everything that same cold, bright glow.

He came to know that glow was the harbinger of visions. Visions of a kind hand brushing away fine black curls, or flashes of brightness and the smell of fear, the taste of blood. He never knew which dream he would get that night, whether it be a comfort or a cruel barrage of painful memories. The different memories swirled together, allowing the nightmares to sour the peaceful respites. Many nights the flurry of images, sounds, and smells woke him to be covered in the acrid stench of sweaty fear.

He was reduced to the same level as an afraid animal. But, still, he pressed onward in preparing for the winter until the smoke had cured the mushrooms, fish, and rabbit meat. And the acorns were submerged in the stream to tumble among themselves and lose their tough outer shell. Their tender inside flesh was then poured into a soft sack to dehydrate throughout his walk.

The wanderer decided to resume walking one fair autumn day. The air was quite warm for the season and the old man felt encouraged by its welcome. He was finally content with his refreshed supply of food for the journey. Packing up everything in his neat, orderly fashion, he set off on his way. The falling leaves danced out of his path as if to guide his boot steps.

At this point in his journey, he was well past his old hunting ground to where he knew where to step. This part of the journey saw him hiking up steeper hills and overpasses. The shrill cry in the distance would warn the old man of the strange elk creature's approach, so he knew to sit undercover and wait patiently for it to pass. The feathery leaves protruding from the thing's shoulders were mirroring the surrounding red-edged yellows. As the creature's ground-rumbling steps led it away, the Traveler's eyes lingered on its shape fading into a mist coming in from the east. Obscurity taking even the largest being in the land and turning it immaterial.

The Snowfall

Continuing the journey over the next mountain, though they were slowly getting smaller in size as the journey went on, proved more than a single day's work for our weary friend. Stopping for rest at its peak allowed for a survey of the path yet traveled. In the years past and the youth he used to have had made the journey seem much shorter before, having a companion also made the journey merrier and less tiresome. Perhaps the air didn't feel so chilly back then. On the grass-covered peak of that mountain, the Traveler built his roaring fire and reclined against a hollow trunk of a dead tree, taking in the sights of the mighty Earth that rolled forth in all directions like a titanic patchwork.

Shadows from the clouds drifted lazily across the landscape. His gaze flickered to meet with the western horizon, where the seemingly endless hills and valleys of green and red would soon meet amber grasses, still months away. The plains would stretch even further than what he could see now on the top of the world. To the north, he spied a great white haze slowly creeping over the dying forest. With it would come winter.

Snow would soon coat the land in lifeless snow; its arrival would stall the wanderer even more with the inclement weather that came with it. Worry began to tumble its way around the corners of the Traveler's reverie like pebbles do an old shoe. He was getting older, more tired, and more than ever he was subject to the whims of the elements. The moisture of winter would dig deep into his joints and make them ache so much that no amount of steamy blackberry leaf tea could remedy. Of course, didn't stop him from trying.

In truth, he found that he quite missed his cottage and the few luxuries it had provided to his simple existence. He knew he would never make it back to his little hermit's respite on the mountaintop; he was choosing where his grave would be. Would it be nestled into his empty little home, sheltered from all the memories of his years? Or would it be alongside a poorly recollected path toward a past that, at best, would yield struggles and dangers that countless lives had spent escaping? And, if somehow, he managed to arrive at his destination, he wondered what he would do. There was no one waiting for him. Only the chance at regaining a long-lost portion of him in an abandoned house by the sea.

A heavy sigh rocked around the empty ribcage of the Traveler, and he exhaled his worries instead of speaking them. His breath came out in a thin mist, as the cold had caught up with him on that hilltop. The lonely one shuffled closer to his fire. Watching the embers flicker against the cool colors lulled him into the sad, desperate sleep of the lost and defeated, dreamless and black. There he floated, resting against that dead tree at the top of the hill where the seasons converged.

The rising sun at his back woke him the next morning, but it was the breeze coming in from the west that got him up. The scent of salt and blue brought with it once more the call to adventure and breathing new life into his muscles. It reminded our companion of the emptiness in his chest and the promise of reclaiming that which belonged to him. In that fleeting moment, his aches dulled, and his burdens felt lighter. This new energy and springiness made his repacking go quickly and his descent down the mountain almost desperate; his path ahead made a little clearer. His burdens are a little lighter.

For all the reviving nature of the scent of childhood; winter came no slower. Two days' worth of travel passed before the Traveler awoke from his slumber to find everything adorned with a fine layer of frost. Even the old man had not been spared the adornment. His bushy, silver beard and eyelashes were encased in the stuff. He imagined he looked quite silly with his gray hair made completely white by the frost.

For all of its charm and amusement, the Traveler had to grimace at its arrival. It meant that the weather wasn't going to get any kinder, and the way forward would soon be entombed in a cold white shell. Nonetheless, he pressed onward, accompanied by a stream that bubbled alongside him. He liked to watch the thing sheets of ice be carried along by the current to catch on the rocks or tumble down a drop. The running water provided some welcome noise that wasn't the Old God's shriek or his own heavy boots.

Almost becoming a sentient companion in itself with its ceaseless chatter. Over the course of the fall, leaves had drifted into the water and submerged beneath its surface.

Forming a river Styx with the unmoving fractals of color in the inky currents like souls paralyzed until judgment. He tried his best to push the thought from his mind. But this omen followed our Traveler with teasing swiftness as it spilled over rocks and twigs.

They only parted ways when it veered South and followed the steepness of the earth into a waterfall, and the old man continued on to the west. Pressing forward, the wanderer noticed the trees taking on a different form. Instead of the merry fullness of short evergreens, their trunks seemed to stretch upward to new heights and kept their branches higher and higher away from the ground below. By now, the leaves had all fallen and the forest was rendered into a skeleton of its former self. The dark trees stuck out like broken bones, reminding the old man of the time he had taken a bad fall and snapped his arm like a twig.

The awkwardness of his arm was reminiscent of the forest he now stood in. Not knowing how to properly tend to the wound, he caught a fever that he wrestled with for weeks. He remembered the smell of his own flesh in that sickness. Both had the loneliness of death clinging to them like a curse. Without the accompanying brook to break the stillness, the silence was deafening.

It commanded respect from those crossing its threshold. The Traveler never spoke much without anyone to talk to, but there is a difference between having nothing to say and being silenced altogether. His footsteps even fell with more care so as to not disturb this yearly graveyard.

After a few days of trekking among the bony limbs of wood, the Traveler began to notice the mist clinging to the area. A curtain of white lazily drifted from the heavens and blanketed the ground in a wet residue. The land was transitioning into its hibernation. The lone figure was the only one not bundling into a warm burrow with a stash of supplies for the winter.

But, still, he trudged on through the wet sludge of rotting leaves and melted snow. The squelching noise of it disturbed the quiet with the uncomfortable sound. That night he laid down whatever dry branches he could find onto the ground beneath his tent to keep the wetness from invading whatever warmth he could muster. They didn't do much; his slumber was filled with murky dreams of an unending swamp with nothing but mud and dead things. He smelled sickness and rot and felt something moving beneath his feet.

He cringed at the stink and jerked awake, frantically batting at invisible creatures in the early hours of the morning. Looking down, he noticed that the wood had done nothing to curb the moisture seeping into his shirt and trousers. Waking to be drenched through with smelly water put him in a sour mood that lasted even as he had changed into the pair of spare clothes from his pack and hung his soiled garments over the fire to dry. He had been wearing his favorite blue shirt, and the idea of the washing he would have to do to it to exorcize the foul odor made him tired from scrubbing already.

When our companion had moods like this, the only remedy was to dip into the precious supply of azure tea with honeysuckle and wait for the tincture to warm him from the inside out. The clothes dried after a couple of hours but remained stiff with a thin layer of muck. He folded them as tightly as he could and wrapped them in linen to prevent them from fouling up the rest of his provisions.

He had to wait until he reached another lake to wash his clothes; the icy waters would be clean enough to get rid of the stench. Rolling the hem of his trousers up around his knees, he waded into the shallows to set himself to scrubbing. He used some valuable soap to coat the fibers in sparse, white bubbles. The suds washed away with the current of the lake, leaving the cloth clean but freezing in his hands. He hustled back to the fire and flung them back over the clothesline to wick away the moisture.

He looked down at his knuckles, numb from cold, and saw they were an angry red. The same with his ankles and shins, he leaned closer to the warmth of the flames before the red would turn to white frostbite. His toes barely moved when he commanded them. As he warmed himself, the feeling began to return to his freezing limbs in a cold burn. He gritted his teeth as he bore with the pain.

At least he could still feel it. One time, when he was young, he saw someone he had crossed paths with suffering from the gangrenous death of flesh from the cold. His feet had turned black and rotten, but when he first saw it, it was washed of all color. Its milky paleness was a sure sign of infectious death.

Though only a boy at the time, he was allowed to watch the amputation while tucked safely under his grandfather's watchful arm. A cautionary tale he had called it. The lesson stuck, and since then he never strayed far from shelter.

He was glad to be rid of the filth that had clung to his clothing; his pack smelled better now. Though unsure of the reason, he had always cringed away from foul smells.

Nothing disgusted him or turned his stomach more than being confronted with sickness and rot. Everything around him had to be clean, especially the fabrics close to his skin. It was with much chagrin that he confronted the possibility of this being his last hope of bathing or laundering for quite a while, at least while the risk for frostbite was so high.

He proved to be correct as the journey crept forward as the air turned frigid with cascading snowflakes and the mist thickened to conceal anywhere but right in front of him. Only the spindly black trunks of the dead trees stood out like freshly inked lettering on a blank page. Any sound halted in its place and was suspended in midair so as to not disturb the sleeping wood. The morning he awoke to this development, he hastened together a pair of woven snowshoes made of leather lashings and whatever flexible branches he could find to bend into the shapes of teardrops. The wide woven flats attached to his boots would allow the Traveler to traverse the deepening snow with ease. His weight now spread out; his legs no longer plunged knee-deep into the snowy dunes around him.

Drifts of softness blurred into each other, not unlike a cold desert. Both had a barrenness about them that allowed the wind to carry its lonely sonnet across the landscape. The Traveler found that trekking through snow in the winter was far easier than struggling in the mush of late fall. Strangely enough, the old man was optimistic about this time of year. Shelter now lay everywhere if he simply learned from the small creatures that somehow thrived this time of year.

When the wind picked up and the soft whistle turned to a roar, he would burrow into the snow and wait out the storm. The trees offered a buffer from the worst of the elements; however, the snow provided a surprisingly comforting abode. The ice cradled its occupant and insulated his warmth until he could fall into a deep slumber. Once the blizzard had cleared, the Traveler pushed fresh, heavy drifts of snow up and aside to emerge into a world bleached by white and glittering with ice. Somehow, the sun had pushed through the thick layer of clouds and illuminated the shimmering realm that had replaced the dreary woodland.

The Traveler sat a moment while eating his dried mushrooms to admire the yearly gifts of jewels the sky showered upon the earth. There was a legend that his grandmother told him when he was small; the sky and the earth were married. Together they created the trees, the animals, and the people too. Through the changes in the seasons, they showed their devotion to each other. In the fall, the earth would show the sky her full colors in a dance of leaves and chill.

Then the winter would come and drape her empty branches with gemstones from the heavens. When they stopped glittering, the ice would melt into the ground and nourish new life to begin the cycle again. If memory served, man also often copied this as an act of devotion. Hard, encased droplets of cold light touching warm skin.

However, such ice wouldn't melt and lacked the life-giving water that the ice and snow would give as it seeped into the soil. In the old man's eyes, the reflection and scattering of light across the snow only really had meaning because of its temporary stay. Such is the way for all beautiful things.

After his meal, the old man strapped his snowshoes to his feet and set about the way forward. The previous weather provided him with a beautiful and enjoyable journey accompanied by sunlight at his back. As his steps carried him forward in the ice, our friend found his previous companion, the babbling stream once again. This time, however, the ensuing freeze had laid a hush over its clamor. Upon closer inspection, the ice had hardened into a translucent shell on the surface of the water.

After standing still for a moment, he could see there was still movement under the lid of the glass coffin. He leaned closer and hovered over the flicker of life. It wasn't much, just a flash of dark green scales in the black waters. But it was life, nonetheless. Such a small sign of existence brought a little bit of comfort to the old man and made him feel a little less lonesome in the world.

Sun continued to bathe his walk with a bright light for the next two days; the snow would melt in the day and refreeze come nightfall. Soon, the ground wasn't crunchy snow but a slippery ice shell over the ground. The fair weather provided encouragement for the adventurer. It wasn't until sundown that the faint whisper of the wind began to pick up into that wintery, desolate howl. Hearing this change in his fortunes and being unable to penetrate the ice, the Traveler hustled desperately in the dropping temperature to find anything on which to brace his shelter.

To his luck, he found a tree before the onslaught took his visibility from him. The best he could then do was forage a few branches to drape his tent canvas over and fling the fresh incoming snow over it. Now much colder, he bundled into the fortified shelter and curled into a shivering ball to get warm again. Growing in pitch, the wind buffed the surrounding trees around as if they were not ancient wood, but fragile reeds. The tent had become half buried by this point, and as a result, the inside darkened and all the Traveler could do was shiver in the cold and dark.

Howling winds continued to beat against the walls, its clamoring cries were the only companion for the being in the tent. Despite his situation, the man did his best to sleep fitfully through what felt like forever but was likely just a couple of days. During that time, all there was to do was huddle deeper into the furs he brought with him and nibble miserably on hard, tasteless food. Only when the shrieks outside abated did he dare to crawl out of his insulation and survey the world around him. Dragging the ice-coated flaps of the entrance aside revealed the world entirely encased in white.

Thick, gray clouds still shielded the fresh snow from the sun, so everything was cast into a gray haze. The stillness of winter cast a hush over the land, making the Traveler that much more isolated. He crawled out of the tent huffing as the chilly air frosted the whiskers on his face and nose. Snow began to wedge itself into the vulnerable gap between his sleeve and glove.

The sudden cold soured the man's mood, and he furiously uncovered the shelter to resume his travels. His frustration added speed and spring to his activity. He stomped angrily over the snow and before very long, found himself quite a way away. It was unclear what time of day it was until a brief gap in the clouds above revealed a sun at the zenith of the winter sky. It would only get darker from here on out, noted the already disgruntled Traveler.

The thing about anger is that anything tints your vision into a dark red color. When you let anger mutate your vision, it's impossible to see anything as its own entity rather than an extension of your wrath. The old man, on this day, was a perfect example of this as he encountered everything as if it was put in his way to increase his troubles. A tree branch was put in his way rather than it just having fallen from its dead trunk. The sudden shriek of the elk creature incoming startled and scared him, and at that moment, he saw the thing as just another obstacle for him to hurtle.

His darkened countenance didn't lighten until fatigue began seeping the fuel of his frustration. For all of the immediate reinvigorations that rage induces, it leaves you more sapped and tired than anything else. It teaches you the consequences of an uneven temper. This lesson weighed on his mind as he set a fire ablaze and settled down for the next night and shed all of the events of the day. He went to sleep that night much humbled and put in his place by his own immature anger. Even in the absence of another being's judgment, his blood flared in his cheeks from the embarrassment of losing his temper.

The next morning shone much kinder than the previous ones, and the Traveler found he woke easier and his bones hurt less from the cold. So resumed his journey forward and into the brighter horizon. Over the course of the following days, he noticed a softness taking place of the bitterness of winter. It was faint, but his skilled nose could pick up traces of green in the air; spring was coming. A glimmer of hope lifted his bushy brow as he came to the joyful realization that he was very close to outlasting yet another winter.

The snow began to melt a few weeks later, the cycle of harsh sun and refreezing nights had created a glossy casing on the ground. Having slipped on these several times over the years, all resulting in different levels of injury, the old man took to carving a branch running his whole height into a walking stick. The beautiful ivory knife danced skillfully in his experienced hands, slicing the bark away to reveal the pale wood beneath. Upon what to carve into the flesh he didn't know. The idea only came to him as he was taking inventory of his stores of food.

He had stopped in a thicket of young aspens to rest for a couple of days and took that opportunity to set traps, giving him the treat of fresh rabbit. With a full belly, inspiration fed a growing idea. That night he set to work carving a rough replica of the cottage he left behind on the bottom of the staff. His new idea and corresponding excitement gave his hands an eagerness that almost drove the blade into his leathery palm. In the absence of paper to document his journey back home, this slender blankness in his hands would serve as a fine substitute.

The work was pleasant and helped the Traveler pass the darker hours of the night huddled by the fire stacked high with logs and spitting embers. It was a fair semblance, the parts he missed the most stood out best. The door and window were a little large for their respective walls. He even etched a little coop into a small mound of unused wood.

While he sliced and dug away at the details each night, he allowed his weary mind to drift absentmindedly back over the peaks of the surrounding mountains. The tundra surrounding the cottage was even drier in the winter, so the snow was always powdery soft and danced as air raced across it. Over the years he had come to enjoy watching the particles of frozen water mix with the wind in a dynamic display of elements. On sleepy mornings by his breakfast table, he would gaze through the window and watch as the elements mingled like merry children. Come to think of it, he hadn't even seen snow until he was a young man.

He had spent his childhood by the churning mass of the sea. The black waters only got colder as the seasons changed, but never solidified into the delicate ice he was surrounded with now. He wondered if he would miss it, the ever-transforming foliage and titanic chunks of prehistoric earth. Once he reached the plains that lay between him and his final destination, he would never again camp among the evergreens were once his home.

Then again, he was going home, wasn't he? Back to the place where he had last felt the warmth in his chest and butterflies in his stomach. He dozed off that night with his thoughts lingering aimlessly through the sky, wandering in between the beginning and end of his travels. As he faded into the inky depths of sleep, he thought of the chickens he had left behind, and whether or not they made it off that mountaintop, and into the safety of the valley below.

The Melt

The days wore on, and the land continued to mollify from its barren whiteness to mushy, wet green and brown as the melting snow seeped deep into the earth and turned dirt to mud. While the rot of fall made him wrinkle his long nose in discontent, the smell of the newly awakened earth was soothing. It reminded the Traveler of his wall of herbs back at the cottage. The scent of new life wafted up from the ground and awoke the little creatures of the forest from their slumber and brought them forth to see their world wiped clean and reborn. Squirrels once again scurried around the trunks of trees once again searching for nuts and seeds to miser and stuff away into their burrows for the next freeze.

The old man thought to himself, *If the chipmunks were the wood's dancers, then birds were its singers.* The Traveler could hear them chirping merrily to each other from the tops of the budding trees, filling the forest with song and bringing it to life. Trees that looked like broken bones and during the winter swayed contentedly in the wind, little buds and new branches reaching out like fingers.

In bearing witness to the reawakening of the world, the Traveler began to notice that with each mile, the earth lay flatter, and there were more and more clearings as opposed to trees. He was getting close to the edge of the woodland and would reach the plains soon. It was a bittersweet moment, perhaps the most dangerous of the journey. He wouldn't be surrounded by plenty and shelter. Out there, he could easily succumb to the elements and exposure. Age only increased that risk. But onward he tread anyway.

With spring came the return of the salty breeze from the Traveler's oceanside origin. The invisible compass rose pointing the way forward. Its fragrance was stronger now than it had been though only by a bit. At this point his stave was already ornately carved with mementos of his journey so far; the cottage, a rabbit, as close as our Traveler could get to recreate the Old God's antlers and the fir trees covered in snow.

The images, however hard old hands worked at it, were a bit misshapen. He barely called himself an artist. But his lack of creativity or eye for the ornate didn't worry him much, as there was no one besides him to see it. The addition of his walking stick made wading through the muck less slippery and the old man's progression advanced quicker than he thought, much to his delight.

After a while, the ground sloped upward in a surprisingly steep hill for the area. The Traveler huffed up its incline until he reached its peak. At the top, the sun pierced through the fluffy clouds like a needle through cotton, and the path ahead was illuminated. A scant few miles and a river lay between our companion and the next chapter of his journey. An ocean of golden plains lay open under an unfurled sky of blue.

His blood rose, and for a moment, he reveled in his victory. It had taken a year, almost a full cycle of the seasons to return to the edge of the rocky top of the world. The waves of earth crashing into each other had been conquered a second time, and now the blank nothingness lay within reach. It would be easier to walk across, but food and resources would be that much scarcer. This weighed on the old man as he carefully descended the hill, his knees barking at him, and made his way through the remaining trees.

He decided to stop midway through to rest once more in the easy shade of the young branches and pillage the bounties of the forest. Much to his glee, the neighboring field housed long stalks of stinging nettles and speckled with yellow dandelion. Taking his sack with him, he harvested their leaves and stalks and carefully laid them out to bake in the sun. Their leaves dried enough to be stuffed back into a pouch for medicinal teas. The excitement of the journey was churning his stomach more than he cared for, and dandelion never failed to settle it.

He chewed on the fresh greens as he promenaded around looking for brambles. A few bushes were blossoming with blackberries, and he couldn't help but pop one in his mouth and pocket the rest. The juices gushed deliciously in between his teeth and over his tongue. He didn't need to look into the reflective surface of the water to know that the inside of his mouth was dyed deep purple. Acorns were still hanging from their branches and had yet to ripen from their pale green to a deep nutty brown, so he found some groundnuts and dug up the roots.

The time he spent filling his reserves served two purposes; he needed to have food for when there would be none, and he needed to wait for the mud to dry enough to walk on. At this time of year, when the rains came, they soaked the ground so much that taking one step was as tiring as taking two. Tiring twice as fast and moving twice as slow wouldn't do at all for the old man, especially when energy came so slowly to him. The years had taken their toll and worn him down, each spring he was finding it harder to recover the strength that the colder months drained from him.

His new campsite gradually became filled with hanging fruits and roots to dry and even a new smokehouse was built to cure the flesh of rabbits and squirrels he trapped. He still had the acorns he had shucked from last season. He didn't like eating raw as much as what he used them for. The kernels had dried out throughout the winter after being stuffed into the bottom of a bag. Now he laid a handful out on a nearby flat rock and began to pound and grind it into a fine powder.

He would first bring a smooth rock crashing down on the kernels, then he would scrape them all together once again and grind them against the rough, flat surface of the boulder he was working on. This took an entire day of steady work that rendered his left shoulder sore for two days. But it was worth it as he poured his finely milled acorn flour into a fine cloth bag to be kept safe until he could use it to make his bread.

After two weeks of this hard work and laden with enough stores to last him for a time, the Traveler set off walking once more. The sun had a chance to dry the earth, and he found that his boots hit the ground with more of a thud than a squelch. There were no more hills to climb, so the distance closed quicker than much of his journey thus far. Something was different about the air today; he couldn't put his finger on it. But as he walked, this burning question hung in the air and dragged with each step.

There is a survival instinct that even humans have, that alerts you to the suspicious nature of a situation even before your other senses have noticed. When your scalp prickles and the sensitive nerves under your skin start to ripple from head to toe. The Traveler stopped in his tracks and let his ears pick up all of the motions of the wood around him.

There was nothing, an absolute silence. He walked on. That feeling persisted and yet there was still nothing: no snapping of twigs that alerted him to a possible stalker, no rumble of the earth as the Old God patrolled his domain, no cry of loneliness. But that was just it.

A cold, slick feeling dropped in inside of the old man at his realization. In the silence of safety was the imminent threat; he hadn't heard the titan that kept crossing his path since that morning. It had been hours since the ground pulsed with its footsteps or the air lit up with its cry. The silence was deafening now; even the birds were quiet. His work had kept him from noticing until now.

His furrowed brow scoured the horizon trying to spot the giant antlers over hulking shoulders. It was only when he looked back toward the mountains he came from that he saw it, unmoving for the first time. It was miles away; its figure shrouded by distance, but there was no mistaking the object of its piercing stare. Its glare traveled the vast miles of wood and undergrowth to meet his. Once again, the old man found himself paralyzed by dread and terror.

His blood drained from his face and head and pooled into his legs. He and the stag creature stared at each other; hollow sockets bored into blue eyes. There was an exchange between the two, at that moment, something unspoken. It had seemed like forever until his legs began to regain their mobility, and he could back away toward the border of the creature's turf.

In the previous interaction with the creature, it had warned him of its knowledge of his presence. Now it felt more like a banishing. It had escorted him safely from its territory in the spirit of seeing him leave as soon as his old bones could carry him. The idea donned on him that there was a reason that larger predators that he usually had to be aware of were strangely out of sight. And that shrill cry had heralded his exit; he had now been sent off to face the rest of the world.

To find his place that didn't infringe on the territory of the new order of giants. That haunting stare emanating from the empty skull was a warning that his footsteps would never again venture over its border. His apparent exile stung for some reason; he had liked to think that he hadn't taken more than his share. His existence in the mountain range hadn't been otherwise offensive or overreaching. Or so he thought, perhaps his kind had simply lingered too long, or taken too much that the earth had remembered and protected what was rightfully hers.

A curious sadness loomed over the Traveler. The thought of the home that he took care of and nurtured over the course of decades being anything, but a loaned patch of wilderness made him feel more lost than ever. It brought back the burning question of whether or not there was a place out there for him at all. The sobriety dulled the remaining walk ahead of him; the stare of the true king of the forest bored into his spine. He reminded himself that he was just traveling through, that he was always just supposed to be traveling through.

Long ago, he wasn't even meant to stay in the mountains, but perhaps cross over to the other side to a destination he no longer knew of. Not knowing where he should go, the only choice was to retrace his steps back to where he last belonged. He was going back to the place of ocean, lavender, and linen curtains. With a renewed resolve, the old man pressed onward to the place where the mountains and trees gave way to the open plains.

White

White is the closest thing to a living thing to any other color. It has a sentience in itself in the way that it dominates. White tints, dims, and infects other colors around it like an overgrown fungus. White descends upon dead things and takes their color away, draining the delicate blushes and green blossoms of life. Everything, at some point, will lose its color into white.

The color of nothing, the color of death. To say it is the color at the end of all things is untrue, due to the fact that white is the end. White conceals what lays beyond like a dense fog and swallows everything into its opacity. Grassy plains, although once golden oceans of tough, enduring flora, reduce into ashen flats of limp stalks when beached white by the sun.

The Traveler gazed across this very wasteland for the first time in many years. Being no more than a child at the beginning of the first crossing, the images of the journey were distorted by time. In his child's eye, the grass looked more golden than it did now. To him the stalks lay broken and limp-looking, more dead than alive. They crunched lightly underfoot as he stepped astutely into the void.

It seemed to him that just in being among so much emptiness, even thoughts began to bake in the dry air. In a few hours, he swore silently to himself that he could see his thoughts dancing just above the skyline like tumbleweeds. They looked like little rabbits, but they were hued blue and purple from the strain that the harsh sunlight put on his eyes. He pulled the brim of his hat tighter over his brow to shield them from the exposure.

Madness lurked in between the grasses like a wildcat and pounced when the heat wore down its prey. The old man had seen insanity descend on past companions. The length of the journey and the displacement had worn away their resolve and left them husks of their former selves. Their reality shifted from the present to somewhere seen only by them. The process by which they lost themselves differed from person to person.

He himself had managed to evade its grasp for as long as he did, he wasn't about to give in to its embrace now. However, he remembered a merry young man he and his grandparents traveled with for a while. Even before the calamity that ended man's reign on the world, life had mistreated him. Still, he had a toothy grin plastered on his face each day. It wasn't until the group had begun to cross the barren void of the plains that the heat showed these misdeeds to him.

Having his trauma played out before him over and over again wiped the smile from his mouth. Being alone with his sorrows rendered him a shell of the happy youth the Traveler had, at one point, looked up to. It ended one day when the young man disappeared entirely. His things remained, but any other trace of him was gone with the winds. The Traveler's grandparents helped him bury his things in a makeshift grave; there would be no body to recover and mourn over. Something his grandmother said over the tomb stayed with him through the years, and he often thought about it when he found himself gazing at the body of a dead animal or tree.

"Into the wild blue, leaving the green and white behind."

He remembered asking her what it meant. He couldn't recall the answer if he ever got one. She had a habit of smiling mysteriously and chuckling softly to herself when he asked these questions. He used to always hate that, it made him feel foolish for even asking. Now, he supposed that it was merely one of those lessons only life and loss can teach. And that made him miss her even more; the wind in his ribs felt all the more empty.

Save for a few herds of small antelope, too quick to hunt for the old man; there was nothing but him and the wind traveling across the plains. It was already late summer, and the flat terrain would provide very little shelter against brutal northern winds. There were no trees to bear the brunt of the elements and the ground would freeze solid before the Traveler had a chance to dig a burrow deep enough. He had the choice of going back to where he was unwelcome and facing the undoubted wrath of the eyeless giant or continuing to push into the improbable. The recollection of the eyeless stare of the elk made him shudder and push onward, bearing this added burden of worry.

The Darkness

With the sacrifice of the mountain scenery came the benefit of an easy walk. The Traveler found the flatness much easier on his aching knees than the rocks and cliffs. Not so much climbing allowed him to advance quickly, or what felt like it, over the landscape. For weeks, he huddled closely around a fire exposed on both flanks. Though unassuming and bleak during the daylight hours, darkness brought with it the terrifying possibility of being spectated. That's at least what he always felt as he clutched his stave to him and piled more dead wood and grass onto the fire.

There were nights that he swore silently to himself that there were glowing eyes circling him as he slept. He remembered a childhood story his grandfather told him once when he had wandered off too far. The great earthen plains around them used to be the floor of an ancient, deep sea. The very sea that stemmed life from its depths. Whenever a whale from the surface died, its body would drift downward to rest upon the sea floor.

There it would be devoured by things not even sunlight could touch. Creatures dyed a milky white and missing their eyes, so accustomed were they to the darkness. In contrast, his grandfather also told him of the glow that some of these things would create. Their very flesh lighting up the black with all of the colors they were deprived of, a twisted rainbow. As a child, the Traveler wondered if the whales ever felt themselves sinking, or felt the bottom feeders nibbling at their flesh in eternal darkness.

Seeing wisps of the colors of the surface dance teasingly among the black. The Traveler remembered not knowing what he would dread most: drowning, being trapped on the bottom of the ocean, or being devoured there in the endless dark and quiet. To feel your strength leave you and be sucked into an endless blue. *It would be horrible*, he thought even now, *to be eaten by things you couldn't see*; only hear their jaws gnawing on his flesh and their teeth clicking together. As a child, he wondered if the souls of those giants were trapped in place.

Or even worse, if there were still the endlessly hungry bottom feeders desperately awaiting a fresh meal. He could only imagine what millennia of starvation would do to them. The fears of childhood crept into his mind as he scanned the darkness surrounding him to spot the flashes of colors that would mark their meal's beginning.

In spite of the terrors that the nights brought him, the old man pushed on during the day. Whenever possible, he would take shelter by a dead tree or rock formation to at least have something to stand between him and the unknown. It was one day when the sun was setting, large and red, by the western horizon that he saw the tiny silhouettes of buildings in the distance. His heart leaped in his chest at the thought of anything with a proper roof.

He was growing tired of the late summer heat; his lips were peeling, and he could tell that the skin on the back of his neck was burned to a crisp. He estimated a day or two of walking before he would arrive. He began to think about the prospect of winter and how he wanted to survive it. Would he change the harshness of the cold or delay his progress for a season?

It was with this question that the Traveler carried with him as he came upon the small collection of sun-bleached, white buildings standing bravely against the bleak horizon. With resigned strides, he hiked into the ruins to take measure the fortitude of the structures. They weren't normal houses, shops perhaps. He could still make out some faint lettering adorning the facades; from them, he derived a grocery store, bike shop, and a hardware store. All of them were empty of products that might have been helpful.

Only shards of dirty glass from broken windows crunched underfoot as the Traveler scanned each desecrated building. In also scavenging for useful items, he was also searching for a suitable place to bunk for the winter. If possible, he would like one with an intact window to look out of and keep away the frost.

As he walked through, he noticed there were barely any signs of human cohabitation other than the buildings themselves. If memory served, bands of desperate pilgrims trying to travel light left few tracks and even fewer objects of use. This dilapidated town likely sheltered wave after wave of pilgrims seeking refuge until it simply had nothing left to give. He thought back to the stare of the mountain elk and remembered the selfish, greedy nature of man, and how the world was left empty by their ceaseless plunder. As a result, there was nothing here to be reclaimed save for a metal pail and a dust-covered book full of faded pictures and even that he took.

At least there was shelter and a small creek that trickled through the town's center. The water was crisp and fresh. He hiked upstream to its source: a small lake a few miles away and up a small hill. The water had carved away at the red stone to create a deep nest for the clear water. It was deep, and if he stood still and watched closely, he could spy the flash of fins and gills beneath its surface.

His spirits brightened at the aspect of a good fishing spot. Before he ventured back to the village, he took his time at the lake and had a bath in the warm water. It felt good to wash the sweaty stink of the heat from his skin. He even spared some of the precious soap to render himself completely clean.

Something about staying in a proper house for the first time in a year of travel made him want to at least act the part of civilized. He re-emerged from the shore of the lake, much refreshed and dressed in fresh clothes. To his own amusement, he found he was standing a little straighter than he normally would, as if being in the presence of human ruins subjected him to discipline.

In his remaining inspection, he discovered that the town and surrounding area proved to be vacant of threats or anything else for that matter. The only sign of life that didn't come from the lone wanderer himself, was an assortment of white tufts of fur strewn about the rundown heaps. The fur was so fine that it almost disintegrated at the slightest touch. This gave him cause for concern being that he no longer had the chaperone of a giant and was now unprotected by the wilds he was in. He remained wary of any peculiar noises or flashes of white but to no avail.

Before long, the Traveler relaxed a bit and even found himself collecting and rolling the hair into a soft ball, enjoying the sensation of touch. The comfort of doing so brought back memories of all the soft things he loved. He remembered a black cat shoving its tiny face into his and piercing the quiet nighttime with its loud contented purrs. Its constant need for attention and affection matched well with a young boy with an aptitude for play and a fondness for small animals.

Sometimes, on the top of the mountain, a red chicken would bustle busily up to him and insist on being picked up and away from the pecks of her neighbors. Something about the feeling of fur and feathers eased his mind when it was troubled. It was with a sadness he knew all too well that he remembered leaving both creatures behind with a door swinging open.

The Church

His walking and fur collecting stopped when one building, in particular, drew his attention and held it fast. A small, denigrated heap of stones and overgrown grass that jutted out like gray, hollow teeth against the horizon. However, none of that managed to disguise its purpose. The Traveler knew what kind of building this used to be. At one point, he recalled, it would have held congregations of people herding around a sage of the god of man. His grandmother had made him go every week, at first he went because he wanted to, only to feel a warmth and comfort take root in his belly and bloom into song through his lungs.

This was before people scattered to the winds and disappeared, leaving the earth to reclaim itself from their wake. When the wars of bygone ages had claimed everything, people yearned for the one thing that could never be pillaged. They would hold each other and lift their voices toward the heavens in joy and loss alike, on the off chance that they were heard. *Perhaps*, he thought to himself now, *being heard wasn't the point*. In the mind of a child, all that he saw was an opportunity to sing with others and take part in the joy of togetherness.

Then again, that is when life bestowed so many gifts upon him. It wasn't until these blessings were revoked that his eyes lifted skyward, and he was desperate to see what they saw. His eyes never enlightened him. But what came back to his tired self now wasn't the sights but the songs. He didn't remember the lyrics, the words that brought the congregation so much hope.

But it was the melody itself that fell heavily on the silence of the empty walls around him. They had sung here, their hopes and fears tumbled together like a gale of summer wind. For years, it tumbled across the sunbaked ground of the barren wasteland until it came back and fell on the ears of the last human, the last pilgrim.

The song filled his lungs until it overflowed up into his throat and out of his eyes. A wet, warm tear overflowed from the eye of the last worshiper and trickled uninterrupted down to his lips. The salt stung as it hit the dry cracks created by the sun. Back at the mountaintop cottage, he remembered what it was like to be lost, and realized that he was. Now he remembered what it was like to be truly alone, making a sad attempt at recreating the hymn's chorus only magnified the empty choir. There was no one to sing with him now, no one to ease his burden of solitude with a forgotten gospel.

How curious to feel such loss at something so vaguely remembered and so invisible and immaterial as faith. To lose something that belonged to you is one thing, over time you forget about it and move along your way. Faith and companionship always come back to you, each time to make fresh in your mind what part of you is missing. And before you can even recall what exactly you are feeling, they leave once again, leaving you that much colder and alone. Nothing ever brings you so high and then brings you so low. So, humming softly the gentle tune to break the loneliness and silence swallowing him, the old man set about taking refuge in this last pillar of the sanctuary.

With the weather turning colder by the day and the incoming frost nipping at his heels, it was time for the Traveler to begin thinking about where to roost for the cold months. Although the thicker stone walls had held up well against the elements over the years, their upright posture seemed to be a miracle. Perhaps this was one last gift from a nameless deity to its lost child, the old man asked himself. Despite being distraught on the outside, the interior of this building showed some promise. The chapel itself was done for; the roof was caved in and the stained-glass windows were shattered.

The scattered shards of color decorated the rotting floorboards with reds, blues, and greens. In the back wall of the chapel stood a thick oaken door that led into a back office, where the sages of old would make their sermons and administer advice. This showed quite a bit of promise. It had at least four standing walls made of stone that would hold stronger than any of the shacks in town. It puzzled him that he hadn't been there before, but somehow understood quite quickly the layout of the old church. See one of them, see all of them, he supposed to himself as he toiled away.

The room had one intact window overlooking the prairie. The glass was filthy and clouded but still intact. The floors were solid wood planks and even had a dirty rug cast over the center of the room. There was a broken desk in the corner and a bookshelf filled with volumes; the old man glanced over them and found that most of them were in a different language he hadn't seen before. He set to work clearing out the space to make it his home.

After dragging out the bits of the desk and stacking the fragments in a neat pile around the back of the exposed wall, he discovered a little stuffed bear tucked carefully in the corner behind where the desk had stood. It was a tiny, pathetic thing, almost too sad to look at. Its eyes were black buttons that had lost their shine eons ago to accumulated filth. Brushing it clean revealed more tufts of soft white fur clinging to the worn gray fabric. Whatever animal had left the fur there spent quite a bit of time with the toy; it was cocooned in the stuff.

He wondered whether it thought the bear was a kind of surrogate child or stand-in parent. That being said, the Traveler couldn't bring himself to throw away something that had, at one time, been held so dearly even if by an unknown animal. As if it was almost routine, the old man remade the little bed and tucked the stuffed animal back into it to continue its dreamless slumber. The Traveler was a bit surprised at his own act of affection toward it. He was never a child that wanted toys or animals; he liked pets most of all, live animals he could mingle and play with.

The limp, sad way that artificial animals just lay there waiting to be played with made him sad. He certainly didn't like their ceaseless staring. But this particular toy found a little cove in his affections and, in the span of a few moments, had made a nest there to curl up. *Perhaps*, he thought, *a child coming through this place had left it to watch over newcomers, would be a shame, a crime even, to take that gift for granted, especially when signs of life were so few and far between.*

As his leathery hands made quick work of the rubble and dirt, he let his mind wander about the walls of the village, mingling with the ghosts. His eagerness made quick work of the room; it quickly transformed from the husk it had been, to the hardy respite of a wayward traveler. The waxy canvas that used to serve as his tent now became a hammock slung into the corner across from the little bear. The age of the church was apparent since there was a cast iron, wood-burning stove already in place, poised to send warmth from wall to wall.

The idea of having a proper cooking apparatus lent an eager energy to the day's chores. He hung his collection of medicines and teas. The acorn flour sack was set on a nail for easy access. After his preparations were finished, all that was left to do was set traps for the winter and wait.

The Refuge

The following week he spent preparing for the months of ice and snow. The walls accumulated his stores of dried meats, combined with his herbs and medicines it became a sad recreation of the mountaintop home he left behind. Rocks and stones mixed with clay-like mud patched the few holes that needled cool air into the room. One benefit to all the ruins around him was that there would be plenty of kindling and fuel for his fire.

Although he did feel a bit guilty over burning the last evidence of the lives people had led here. He relished the last of the fall and fished each day in the little lake to dine on fresh meat that night. His shortening days drifting by in relative ease and comfort.

The temperature of the wind began its steady decline. He was outside clearing the floors of the surrounding buildings in an effort to somewhat beautify the scenery when a snowflake drifted down and rested on the exposed top of his hand. The sudden cold surprised him, and he stared blankly at the lacy architecture as it melted into his tanned skin.

It was more rounded than straight, with little plumes of frost pushing outward of a fractal center. It was cold, but not bitingly so, just a nip of chill. However, its arrival meant that the hard, hungry times were close behind it. With a sigh, the Traveler embraced the harbinger's grim message and finished his day's work.

After each day of tidying up the village of its trash and pillaging the surrounding hunting grounds, the lonely one sank into his fireside hammock and cooked his meals. It felt nice, having the sounds and smells of a hot meal heating up over the glossy black stove. Little by little, the lonely little room felt like home. The building seemed to rejoice in being inhabited once more.

The stones warmed and gave off their residual heat when the fire died down low. Nights were becoming easier for the old man; the paranoia was subsiding the longer he dwelled within strong walls and tucked away from peering eyes. That being said, he still found himself darting glances over his shoulder whenever the bright sky began to fade, and the darkness approached.

During these evenings of rest, he often found his fingers fidgeting at the worn corners of the dusty photo album in boredom. The book was bound in an obnoxious shade of fuchsia cotton. In poorly drawn purple letters on the front spelled "Beth," and the ends of each of the letters were tipped with faded, dirty stickers. The pictures were damaged by water, and tinted sepia, but his eyes could still make out the images. His back ached as he hunched over the album and eagerly flipped through the first few pages. Almost like a portal into someone else's mind and eye.

The first few were rather mundane, a white house by a road, happy-looking people, and a muddy dog. Everything was hard to make out due to the photographer's shaky grip on the camera. More often than not, the actual subject was blurred and unfocused, and the only clearly visible thing was a wisp of auburn hair or a misplaced thumb. Sometimes he would catch a glimpse of the terrain the family was living in, a valley of rocks and thorny bushes with mountains high on all sides.

Everything was gray and somber, a direct contrast to the lush green that the Traveler had just left, and the blue salty place he was going to. If anything, it seemed to him that it was merely a different tone of plains. Mimicking its emptiness, only with different colors. He wondered to himself which direction they had come from.

The old man, not wanting to spoil the only new source of amusement within hundreds of miles, tucked the album away into an empty pocket of his canvas bag and brought out the old book that used to work as a level for his table. His grandfather used to read it to him before bed, and if he was still in the world, he would have scorned him silly for abusing it. Somehow, doing those little things that would have made him cross or upset reinforced the echoes of his presence. Grasping at straws really, but when you are so alone as he was, you do strange things to ease that heavy burden. Now, however, he dusted it off and looked carefully at the cover.

It was a paperback, with the spine well-bent and the pages dog-eared, a bad habit of his grandfather's. When he read, he would hold it in one hand and bend the sides back around itself to read a page. As a result, the art on the cover was ruined by a ripple of tan where the weathered paper tore. What had been there once was an image of a dense green forest with a tower looming above it, and descending into the darkest parts of it was a tiny figure radiating golden light. He had spent his childhood being read to from this book but had never fully paid attention before falling asleep.

Perhaps this time he could fully grasp the narrative and see what his grandfather saw in it for the last few years he spent scanning through its pages. The Traveler flipped it around and looked at the synopsis on the back. It spoke of a shimmering tower and a decrepit city on the edge of the world though in the same space, never at the same time. And the fates that interwove within each other like a spider's web. Like many stories, there was a hero in the beginning, a child with nothing but a lantern and a self-imposed quest.

The Traveler only read the first chapter that night, wherein the child, named Marx, left his sleepy hometown to pursue the call to adventure with his pet sparrow. He lived in a sleepy town by a silver lake; all was safe and quiet. The day's beginning saw the little boy absentmindedly putting fireflies in a jar and hanging it by his door and ended with him journeying into the endless forest following the gentle singing voice of his lost mother. His hope of reunion was a tiny, weak light against the domineering onyx darkness of the unknown.

It was a story full of nonsense and eccentric ideas, the old man thought. It seemed to him more of a story for children than something a grown man would enjoy. His grandfather read it to him, but he seemed to gain more enjoyment out of it himself. He supposed to himself that he would find out the deeper into the book he read. The Traveler leaned back with a tired sigh, sinking deeper into the hammock, and looked blankly at the pages before him.

Perhaps the boy Marx would grow into a sort of traveler himself. They were not dissimilar, the two, both were following breadcrumbs left by mysterious voices of the past, hoping for revelation. That being said, our Traveler had no sparrow to bring the comfort of lonely nights, only the brisk wind of the great plains. He sighed again and closed the book with a dull thump that puffed dust into the air. He paused for a moment longer and watched the particles reflect the amber afterglow of the stove fire. If he did not know they were dust and filth, he would think them to be beautiful with their otherworldly slow drift to the ground.

The Dreams

Dozing off into a hard sleep, the lonely one dreamed of warm summer sun and cool updrafts of ocean breeze. He caught glimpses of a being nestled into a bed of sweet-smelling linens. The familiar salty air wafting through that small window made of clean glass. Looking out, the Traveler saw gray sand and the white-trimmed blue of the sea. He remembered its waves crashing into the shore relentlessly like the daily cry of the elk king in the mountains.

He remembered his younger self running along the grainy sand, hearing the deliciously satisfying crunch underfoot and the icy waters tickling his toes. The mysterious fold and pull motions of the waves before they receded back into the greater mass. His small ears rang with laughter and delighted shrieks echoing from every direction, the chaos of fun. This was quite the noisy dream, the ambiance swallowing even thought. Only allowing for mindless bliss in the motion of the day.

But through all the sounds came one gentle, whispered voice that held the dreamer's attention. He heard no words, only the warm breath on his ear, and made out a crooked smile that mirrored his own. The smell of lavender filled his lungs, and he now recognized the face before him. He craned his neck to see more of her face: her ashen hair, the smile lines around her eyes in her tanned skin. Her words were killed by a sudden, piercing whistle and a flurry of snow on his face.

Dreams are so cruel like that; they exist to remind us of the sorrows and faults of waking. To dream of comfort only makes waking that much harder when you know that bitter cold and hunger await you. And wake he did, as the crashing of water turned to howls of wind. One of the corners that he had reinforced must have come apart to expose the interior to the gales of a midnight blizzard. Not wanting to lose what heat had managed to linger in the four walls of the sanctuary, the old man bustled hurriedly about the space gathering pebbles and grasping for a pelt.

He stuffed them into the hole in the corner to reinsulate it and halt the influx of freezing air. His makeshift plug held fast, but it was too late; the room was reduced to an icebox. Shivering, the Traveler piled some more wood onto the dying fire, stuffing the wood clumsily into the stove. The embers flared a dull red, and heat began to radiate again. He bundled back under the piled pelts and linens he had atop the hammock to conserve whatever warmth he could muster.

He lay there for about an hour, his body shaking in the silence, impatient for comfort. Gradually, whether by the heat of the reignited fire or by the friction of his shuddering, he became warm once again. He shut his eyes and chased once again after the dream, only for it to hover just beyond his reach. He lay there attempting to recall the images of that joy, only for the faint rustling in the far corner to disturb him.

The Animal

A strange shuffling kept disturbing the silence, keeping the Traveler from reaching the refuge of slumber. At first, he thought it was nothing more than the stones settling, or some leaves he had missed in his cleanup being agitated by another leak. Realizing the likelihood of an unexpected visitor, the sleeper froze and glared around the room under a bushy gray brow. It took a moment for his eyes to adjust enough to pierce the darkness and see the source of the sounds. It was in the corner, the one with the stuffed bear, a small figure was wriggling into the surrounding shadows.

While the creature shrank desperately into space in an attempt to disappear from the man's line of sight. The Traveler stood up quickly to tower over the thing. The thing squealed in response to his movement. Reaching out with his burly, knotted fingers, he snatched at the ragged ball. It had a long body that wriggled and squirmed at his grasp, but once he got a good hold on the matted fur, he raised it to the light to see.

It was more fur and bone than an actual animal; ribs poked through its dirty hide. A pointed nose covered in black fur and white whiskers protruded from its head, and it thrashed its tiny jaws at him, revealing tiny yellow teeth in crooked rows. The thing was so weak and ragged that all it could really do was bat weakly at the large hand gripping it by the scruff of its neck. After deciding that its worn teeth and scrawny legs posed no threat, he dropped it gently back onto the dirt floor.

This creature confused the Traveler, it didn't look like any fox or wildcat that he had encountered. The length of its furry torso was very weasel-like and the hissing sounded like an angry cat. It must have come in through the weaker corner seeking shelter from the storm. The sad mass of fur cowered away from the tall figure before it and hissed weakly into the ragged neck of the teddy; whether protectively or in pursuit of protection, the man didn't know. Didn't quite know why he cared either.

Anything this small and pathetic wouldn't survive outside with the gales howling like they were. Despite his distaste for feral, dirty creatures in his sleeping quarters, the old man let the creature be. The thought of chasing it out into the maw outside seemed unnecessarily cruel. He measured that it would either be gone on its own by the light of day or that he would, at least, have an idea of what he wanted to do with it.

Once again, the wanderer crawled back into the respite of blankets to hibernate the coldest parts of the night away. There were no more dreams, only the peaceful nothingness that comes with fatigue. He woke that morning to the eerie glow of a blizzard through the window. The flurry obscured everything from sight and only left the cold, haunting empty. However, the light was light, and it illuminated the room without him needing to use excess fuel.

It was cold that morning, so he stoked the flames and fed them anew anyway. The corner where the thing was hiding was quiet, so the man did as he pleased and set about making his breakfast. He ducked outside to fill the metal bucket he had found with snow. The cold was shocking, and he reentered the room gasping at the air stolen from his lungs and his nose hair frozen uncomfortably. He placed his newly acquired snowballs in the ceramic pan he brought with him and set it on top of the black metal stovetop.

The white balls shrank into clear water. Using extreme care and caution not to spill, he scooped a handful of acorn flour from the sack on the wall. Over the summer, the stave was not the only thing that he had carved, but also a bowl and a plate fashioned from a tree branch before he left the forest. The wooden platter came in handy as he mixed the flour with bits of water until it formed a soft, lumpy dough. On the mountaintop, he took his time with the baking and allowed the dough to rise.

Now, all he wanted was fresh, hot food. So what he did was roll it delicately out with a smooth part of his stave until they formed thin flat loaves; they would not rise since he had left his starter behind. He missed the ripe smell of the fermented mass since, to him, the aroma smelled of the comforts of home. He threw these new, more disappointing loaves onto the hotter surfaces of the stove to cook through. He then plucked some dried meat and mushrooms from their bundles and threw them into the small cast iron he had brought with him. A little more water, and then it began rendering out the tender flavors that still lingered in the fibers.

An earthy, savory smell filled the room and the old man found himself thinking of home once more. As his breakfast sizzled in the glossy metal pan, The Traveler's eye flicked toward the corner with the small gray thing from the other night. It was still there, sorrowful and shivering against its only friend. A hollow feeling knocked around the inside of his ribcage as he recalled the now-empty chicken coop at home. Something about pitiful creatures being left to the chaotic laws of nature curdled something deep in his gut.

The food that should have been juicy and succulent now weighed like tasteless clay on top of his tongue. The taste mingled with the sense of guilt until the Traveler found himself offering up a small morsel of hare meat to it, anything to ease the sour heaviness of this feeling. Nothing could entice the creature enough to overcome the ruling fear, however.

The old man sighed and gave up on having the animal get past the manhandling he had given it that night, the old man left the sustenance within crawling distance of it. *Not that he could blame it*, he thought to himself, *he'd be furious to be lifted into the air like he was nothing*. He left it to the dank draftiness of the corner to sulk and retreated back to don his coat, as there was still work to be done.

The dislodged rock on the outside had to be replaced before the blizzard reached its climax. Once outside, the sleet came close to blinding the old man. Instead of the friendly, fluffy snowflakes of the winter's very beginning, it came down hard and swiftly. It pelted any vulnerable skin, and even in the areas he thought most secure by leather and fur; the flurry wedged itself tightly into a crack to rest upon his skin. Nothing like a blizzard to tell you where your coat needs repair, he thought grumpily.

Still, he pressed forward with one hand on the icy stones to guide him. He felt his way around the structure; the steel toe of his boot caught on a loose rock here and there until he found what he was looking for. The hole in the corner of his hut, the creature likely burrowed desperately in to get at the warmth and light. Shockingly strong for its stature, the rocks were heavy, and the clay he had used as mortar had dried solid. It had managed to pry all of that loose and wriggle its way to the inside.

His knotted hands felt around again for the misplaced stone and wedged it back into the gap. In the absence of the clay, he packed snow around it to seal the entrance. When he was content with the new seal, he felt his way back along the freezing stone walls until he reached the solid oak door. Before he scrambled back through the threshold, he scooped a handful of fresh snow and brought it in with him.

The room was quieter now that the hole was sealed better and much warmer too. The snow in his hand was melting and dripping icy water through his gloves and into his palm, numbing the skin. He plopped it into the small pot and slowly peeled off his many warm layers. His overcoat, scarves, gloves, and jacket all went on nails in the wall to dry and warm. Their hems dripped water as the snow on them melted.

He slipped off his boots and wiggled his toes in their thick woolen socks. He had knitted them himself, a skill he took no small amount of pride in. Years before, in his mountain home, he had come upon a village from which he could pilfer resources unavailable to him in the natural world. There he could find his tools and even protective clothing. The cans of food in the grocery store had long since expired and gone foul, but he could still get the occasional materials.

He even found that the little town had a fabric store, stacked floor to wall with multicolored yarns and fabrics. His favorite of which was a thick spool of soft, dark blue yarn with a smooth feel. The socks he looked at now were made of just such a material, the deep, intense color a welcome change from all the bleached sky surrounding him. He focused on them, trying to infuse the energy and life of their color into himself. During the winter, it was hard to not let the entombing white drain him of his own hue.

His reverie was interrupted by the sound of soft bubbling; the snow had melted and now jumped about the pot with a newfound life. He took it off the heat and let the surface settle, no longer the aggressive rolling boil it had been. Taking a small bit of stinging nettle, he dropped the dried husks into a soft little sack and bobbed it into the hot water.

The pleasing aura of the tea seemed to warm the inhabitants and even the creature on the corner ceased its tense shivering for a while. The Traveler poured the contents of the pot into his copper cup and lowered himself onto the overturned tin pail. His mind lulled by the comfort of the steamy warmth, and he found himself slipping easily into a drowsy haze.

There was still a bit of food remaining in the pan, now gone lukewarm with neglect. It tasted better now with his improved mood. The subtle flavors of the forest took him back to the moss-covered summer and the golden fall. The only things missing were his peppers, he thought wistfully. He enjoyed the spicy sweetness they added to each dish.

Visions of the egg he had before his departure danced in his mind's eye. He imagined its orange yolk spilling slowly over the bread and imbuing everything in its thick luxury. The bite of the salt came through all that heaviness and mingling merrily among all the flavors. Nonetheless, he ate this much sadder meal at his own pace, still grateful that he had food to fill his belly, and once he was finished, he neatly cleaned the small space and settled in to wait out the harshness of the weather. Sometimes, when he was putting off a task to be done or simply had an hour or two to spare, he let his mind drift about the road he had traveled.

He found he enjoyed the thought of himself hovering above his body and flying through the sky on a gust of wind, surveying the path yet traveled. The old man dwindled in this half-present state for about a time but came back down to himself when the sky turned from white to gray. Hunger eluded him, so he didn't think it necessary to dip back into his stores. He instead reached into his pack and brought out the faded, dog-eared book for another chapter of the child-traveler Marx and his ongoing venture into the black woods.

The forest loomed over the young Marx and his sparrow. Illuminated only by the guiding light of his small lantern, he followed the guiding whisper of the long-lost mother weaving through branches and brush. It appeared to him almost like tiny strings of wispy red hair leading down a narrow path through the dense wood. His short legs tripped over an overgrown root on the ground and the little light he had shattered on the rocks. Succumbing to hopelessness so soon on his journey, the little boy Marx cried at the loss of his last comforts.

Suddenly, the flashes of auburn reappeared and surrounded the boy with a golden glow. He heard his mother's soft call and gentle singing voice. She sang of hills and valleys and the joys of family and Marx found his somber heart lifted at the sound of the lullaby. Blinking away tears he slipped into a slumber protected by a ring of song and red hair. When he awoke, the forest was quiet, but he found a new light had taken refuge in his broken lantern, emitting a golden-red aura.

Much more cheerful at this gift, the child walked ever farther into the dark. His faithful sparrow circled his bouncy head like a golden-brown coronal. Singing this same lullaby to pass the time, Marx skipped and pranced through a newly tamed woodland. The shadows gave way to the new magical lantern his mother had given him. And onward he strode toward the forest's dark center.

The chapter ended with that, the unapologetic tease of a new adventure. The old man pondered on the meaning of the sparrow. He had tried a few times throughout his long life to domesticate a bird for a pet. Only to have them nervously peck at his offerings and flit away once they had their fill. He figured that perhaps a small child was less of a threat.

The closest he ever got to a feathered friend was a crow that brought him a leaf once. And even then, he only did it in exchange for a slice of bread and then flapped away on his black wings with a screech. The kind of animals that warmed up to the Traveler tended to be bigger and lazier in nature. Deer would eat from his hand nervously while eyeing him; sometimes, a fox would let him pet it. Back when he himself was small, not unlike Marx, he had a tiny ball of black softness from which gazed suspicious, green eyes.

Quite shapeless it was, he recalled silently, nothing more than a moving shadow that only took form when reaching out his thin paws to swipe at his toys. Thinking of those eyes, the Traveler glanced toward the tiny animal in the corner. It was still there in a ball next to the stuffed bear, flinching at each new gust of wind. Its gaze was glued to the Traveler. Its beady eyes were dark like the black waters of a midnight lake, glittering intelligently. It was the kind of dark that saw everything; no matter where you moved, it always saw you and reflected, coldly, back your own gaze.

The firelight stove reflected off of the obsidian spheres, giving them a yellow glow in of themselves. The food he had left out was gone at the very least, so it wasn't starving anymore. The two sat there, staring blankly at one another nervously. Black eyes meeting blue. It seemed like forever until one of them broke the spell and an uneasy truce was formed.

Allowing his attention to fall away from the thing, the Traveler picked the photo album up and resumed scanning their beaten pages. This time, the pictures consisted of a car piled high with belongings; a journey was underway. A blurry glimpse of the father revealed a brow carved into a worried expression. Pictures of the mother showed a forced, straining smile which seemed to be for the benefit of the small photographer, as the images always showed her looking straight at the lens. These expressions were subtle so much so that anyone who didn't scour the page with their eyes would just think that she was posing for another photograph.

But the old man knew that look; he was very familiar with the hawk-like watch of a guardian. This little girl's mother wasn't letting her beyond her protective reach. Another snapshot revealed the contents of the child's backpack; the photo album itself wedged among picture books. The cover was much cleaner but still the same ridiculous shade of pink. The stickers were crisp and new, however. They had butterflies and flowers on them.

The next page continued to show a long, seemingly endless dirt road surrounded by plains; there was a fairly large chance that those were the same flats that the Traveler, himself, was surrounded by. In absent-minded curiosity, he wondered which direction they had come from. And how they had ended up here where he was now. He found it strangely comforting; a wanderer is perhaps not so lonely if he is traveling the path marked by other footprints. It was a pleasant thought, despite the fact that the child had likely passed through here only briefly and to greener fields.

If that little family survived the long journey. Flipping further forward into the album, only more jumbled images of the vacuous open space. Pictures of another family all cramped in the car with their belongings, perhaps neighbors. There was a final picture that showed the brown dog sitting sadly in front of the house. It had lanky limbs and a mournfully long face.

There were a few images of this, each of them smaller as the car took the family away, leaving their furry friend behind. Continuing on, the parents still donned their worried expressions as their heads leaned toward one another, giving the old man the impression that they weren't mere vacationers but had uprooted their little family and left behind the dog for a reason. A rather pressing one. The Traveler recalled dimly having been on such a journey as a child. The adults rushed around, packing whatever would fit, and stuffing their loved ones into trailers and trucks to escape a coming cataclysm.

That same worried shadow was cloaked by the supposed excitement of it all. The aspect of adventure and somewhere new took precedence over the sadness and fear of what was left behind. He could recall seeing other families and other children. They played together when they could; he couldn't remember any dogs though.

Nevertheless, the Traveler wondered if he had ever crossed paths with the family in the pictures. He liked to think that he had. The new mystery weighed heavily on his mind as he put away the photos and set about carving more of his journey into his stave.

By now, his hands had transformed a third of the staff into a chronicle of his exploits. Blades of wavy grass bloomed from the carved antlers of the behemoth of the mountains. During his long walk across the ocean of land, he had added some mushrooms to the images, and stemming from their round caps, he whittled the broken-down horizon of the village. The steeple of the church still pierced the huge prairie sky. The cold was soaking his fingers with a dull ache that made manipulating the blade clumsy and slow.

By the time he laid down the stave and dusted the shavings of his project from his trousers, his knuckles seemed to creak when they moved. But it was work he was happy to do, having something to do with his hands felt good to the soul, if not to his joints. He was used to always working with his hands in caring for the plants and animals by his little cottage.

There wasn't a day that he wasn't tilling some soil, chipping away at some household repairs, or tidying the muck of his poultry. Now his hands seemed to twitch from the neglect and itch from the stillness. And the boredom of the winter months would soon weather away his sanity without something to tweak with the hands and focus the eye.

As he toiled with the knife and wood, he found that time was flowing like water around the walls of the room, and before he knew it, the sky had darkened into its black opacity. The grumbling of his stomach informed him of his own hunger. So, he set about making his evening meal, but out of the corner of his eye, he saw his little companion sniffing nervously from the shadows. Its black eyes twitched from him to the food in his hands. *If he was hungry,* he thought to himself, *then this poor creature must be ten times that.*

This night's meal was a soup of sorts, the broth made of water and whatever ingredients steeped into it. It was thin, but he drank it gladly, as it filled his belly while preserving the stockpiles that he had. Normally, he would be able to still hunt and trap this time of year, but the unceasing gales of sleet and snow made that a danger he couldn't risk. If he got lost out in that cold, he would never make it back. Not at his age.

So for now, what he had with him would have to do until the blizzard let up. That being said, he could only take the forlorn look of the thing in the corner for so long until he poured an extra portion into a small bowl and set it before the beast. He saw the hunger take over the fear as it lapped greedily at the soupy food and wriggled into the safety of its inanimate friend. All three of them soon succumbed to sleep in the midst of the harsh storm outside the walls of their only respite.

The next few days passed just like that, blending into the somewhat hibernating nature of winter existence. The Traveler would wake and prepare a meager meal for himself and the little thing in the corner. It would always flinch away until it was sure he was there only to deliver food and nothing more. However, after a couple of routines of this, its small sharp nose began to poke around the Traveler's pack and at the bundles of dried herbs and plants on the walls. Its movement, although tense at first, was welcome among all of the dead winter stillness.

He let it do as it pleased and settled back into his hammock naps with the photo album or book on his chest. The two began to tolerate one another's company. Loneliness was the most unlikely of unifiers. Eventually, the thing, which the old man called Bear in his own mind, would eat tentatively out of his hand with a twitchy nose and watchful eye. Its short, nervous breaths tickled the Traveler's rough palm, a sensation similar to when a small deer or fox would sniff at his offerings back in the mountains.

It was surprising to him to miss this feeling, the comfort of another living thing, if this creature could be called that. He was surprised that it had made it this far for this long. Tiny ribs poked through the dirty fur, mirrored by those of our Traveler; *there was not enough saved food to fatten either of them up,* he thought grimly. He glanced out the window and saw what he had hoped to see. Between the gusts of wind, he could see farther than he used to; he could make out the shapes of the village. The snow was thinning. He now dared to hope to be able to venture out.

The Warmth

When the wind wasn't so ferocious and the sun bore down on the ashen ground, the Traveler peeked his head out through the door. The icy wind ruffled his gray hair, still losing whatever color remained. The sun was bright and cold but had stopped the gales of wind carrying more snow. The Traveler dared to leave his shelter to set traps and hike up to the frozen lake to fish. Any fresh meat was welcome.

Despite their usefulness and longevity, dried food wore down his jaw most of the time, and decades of living wild on the land hadn't been kind to his teeth. He found he longed for something soft and tender to savor. So he waited patiently by the hole he cut in the lake's frozen surface for the line to tug. It didn't take very long; the fish underneath were probably just as eager for fresh food as he was. When he returned, he saw that in his absence, Bear had slithered its long slinky body into the mass of blankets in the hammock.

The ever-present teddy hoisted next to it as it slept in the lingering warmth. The old man was less than pleased at this development because of the filth clinging to its fur. It clearly wasn't afraid of him anymore, so he could now expect this boldness more and more. He looked over it pensively, and with a sigh, left with the pail to gather snow.

When he arrived back with the bucket filled to the brim with crunchy white, Bear was awake and staring at him with those beady black eyes. Measuring him up and trying to calculate what was going to happen next, it knew that dinnertime was a few hours away still. Its anxiety filled the room as it watched the snow disintegrate. There was a newfound tension in the small room as the snow melted into cold water and warmed as the old man pulled his soap out of his pack. Despite its apparent intelligence, Bear didn't quite understand what was happening and what the yellow bar in his hand meant until the Traveler had already taken firm hold of the scruff of its neck.

He began slowly petting the dirty fur with the wetted bar of soap until the thing was covered in a greasy residue. He had to take great care not to get the creature too wet or the cold would still penetrate the mess of fur and freeze the small animal. As gently as he could manage, he dipped his hands into the water bucket and worked the soap into a lather. What normally were white-ish bubbles were now a dark gray-brown as the dirt was shaken loose from the creature's hide. Bear didn't quite like this, it put up a protest, but once it saw there was no escape, it settled down grumpily. It took longer than the old man had hoped to wash all the dirt from the fine fur; he was worried that Bear might freeze or protest if he took too long.

It took three or four times with the water to rinse out all the soap from the fine fur, which was now revealed to be white. When he was done, he was taken aback by the new prettiness of the animal. Bear was a sleek, white weasel-like creature with a dark face and ashen whiskers, a bit bigger than he had thought.

She, as she was revealed to be, only stayed still long enough to be dried roughly with a brown cloth close to the fire. Then once the old man let her go, Bear darted over to the teddy and dragged it by the leg over to the fireside. Her black eyes glittered with silent fury as she warmed herself by the fire and let her pearlescent coat dry. The white gave off an afterglow from the yellow flames. He let her wallow in her own bad mood and merely studied her curious appearance.

In his lengthy and close-up experience with animals all over the land, he had traveled. Never before had he seen a mix of characteristics such as hers. Of course, it wasn't out of the ordinary for strange things to occur in this newly claimed world. When humanity was gone, all sorts of strangeness rose from the ground. It wasn't out of the realm of possibility that this was of the same curious origins as the great Elk God from the peaks.

Hardly of the same ilk, he thought, one was half the size of a mountain and the other barely came up to his shins. The Traveler pondered this as he dumped the brown water outside; her gaze digging into his back.

So continued a full week until the two cabinmates had reached another, new kind of truce. Many hours were spent uneasily staring at one another. Bear reluctantly took the food he offered, less so when he managed to get fresh fish or a smaller mammal. Her favorite seemed to be the former. She devoured it with relish whenever he came home with the slippery game on his line.

He could spy her following him out to the lake sometimes. The company was welcome, and it lightened his mood to see her frolic on the ice and peer at the fishing hole. Over time, the two grew closer and more at ease in the presence of the other. One particularly cold, windy night, the Traveler felt a small, shivering mass wriggle its way into the warm bundle in the hammock with him. She had, of course, dragged her teddy with it.

The Traveler could feel her slight little frame burrow against his side, where most of the warmth was. Her tiny claws scratched him gently, and she made her new bed at his side. Surprised at this development, there was nothing for him to do other than shift carefully to allow the creature to wrap herself back around the bear and wait for the stillness of sleep to take them both.

That following morning, breakfast was enjoyed together by the fire in a newfound kinship in warmth. Bear had perched herself beneath the crook of his knee and watched him prepare his tea. He used the blue petals this time, their mild sweetness filled his belly with the comforts and promises of spring. Spring was still a few months away, but it was on cold, white days that he reserved that promise of bloom to remind him that however harsh the winter or cold the wind, snow would always melt and the seasons of plenty would return. That day he gave himself a few chores to do, to pass the time.

As comforting as Bear was now to his lonely days, she produced an awful lot of shedding. The mystery of the white tufts of fur appeared to be solved; the fur was everywhere. Why she had devolved into such a pathetic condition was another matter, entirely. The old man refilled the pail with snow and melted it down to clean the brown cloth he had used to dry off Bear. After that, he once again refilled the snow and melted it down to water.

Using the same coarse brown cloth, he carefully and meticulously scrubbed and polished the walls and floor where the dust was collecting and tinting the whitewash and wood flooring gray. Once he was done, he burned dried sage leaves to smoke out any impure air that might have lingered. The stuff stank, but the air had a crisper quality to it once the delicate tendrils of white translucence seeped into the materials of the room. After that, the old man stung up a rope from one corner of the ceiling to another. Over that went his linens and blankets to air out and absorb yet more smelly sage.

Proper laundering was impractical when any water would retain the cold and freeze. The best he could do for now was allow the air to freshen the fibers to a degree. Chores, for some reason, seemed to lay a blanket of calmness over the room. The walls were now a clean white, and the floors shone with the aged wood once more. The simple acts of neatening up and clearing the air made any space, no matter how foreign, seem a bit more like home.

His spirits lifted a bit, the old man began humming that same hymn he remembered from childhood Sundays. Bear sat lazily in the empty hammock, watching him carry out his duties. Comfort suited her, when she was relaxed and peaceful, it was easier to glean that same feeling from the air around her.

That day passed quickly with the tasks at hand. Although it was lovely outside; the sky stretched out in all directions in a magnificent blue. Once the hammock was once again covered in blankets and the fire was roasting dinner, the Traveler allowed himself the simple pleasure of stepping outside into the cold to watch the sky turn from bright periwinkle to violet. The atmosphere was staining itself with the deep, somber colors of twilight. Wisps of the daytime colors flickered weakly at the horizon, waiting to be overtaken by the ensuing darkness.

The old man found that he could see his favorite color here, nestled in between the peach and indigo. A special, sweet vibrancy of lime green was the last color to give way to the void of night. He thought green was the most spirited of colors, the way it was present everywhere that sprouted life. It reminded him of the good months when food was plenty, and the sky sang with life and activity. Yet now his absolute favorite was the color that flashed just before the witching hours descended.

The sun disappeared behind the horizon and left the world devoid of light once more, and as the sky deepened even further from purple to black, he retreated to the safe confines of the room and left the strangeness of the night to its own devices. Bear sleepily blinking at him from her favorite spot on the hammock; at this point, he could read her expression as easily as his own. She was waiting for him to prepare dinner. More dried roots and tough jerky.

The Sickness

As the days further shortened deeper into the throes of winter, the two cabinmates found themselves drawing closer when the winds rose to beat hard against the window and door. Sometimes the wind would reach such a pitch that it was a wonder in itself that the church didn't come down around them. The gales howled like banshees in their perverse songs of loss and hardship. The old man dreaded this more than anything; even at the top of his mountain, there were winds like this. When you live so long in solitude, without another person to speak to, or hear their voice, anything sounds like a human.

These winds would howl and screech in the deepest hours of night, waking the old man to the sounds of terrified people running from fate. He had nightmares whenever this happened, giving him a fear of sleep. So, when each morning saw the sun came out from behind the faraway mountain range, it illuminated the purple bags under his eyes. Bear sensed his anxiety and took residence by his head. Her soft breathing was a small comfort, the gentleness a stark contrast to the wildness of the outside weather.

Dining together on his forage and hunting efforts. Despite the very modest amounts that the Traveler fed her, he noticed that Bear stood a bit bigger than she had before. Her slight frame grew petite cords of muscle under the fine fur. She was still a skittish little coward, but it warmed the old man to see the small flicker of life growing.

Each night, the Traveler would flip a couple more pages of the album, pondering on the pictures and memories of the little stranger. There were dozens of pictures of the plains, perhaps the child saw something she wished to capture but couldn't work the camera to her advantage. Unfortunately, all the bleached photos revealed was an equally bleached flatland as dull as it could be. It took a couple of pages of this to finally come upon something the Traveler could recognize. In the faded edge of a picture containing sleeping bags being set up around a fire was the teddy bear.

It was newer and in better shape but remained the same bear. The creature's namesake was tucked into the small pink sleeping bag awaiting sleep. Its vacant button eyes staring somewhere away from the white borders of the photograph. A withered smirk cracked the ever-silent mouth of the old man, pleased at the piecing together of the puzzle. Moving on, the town came into view, still as white and broken down as the one housing him now.

The church, however, was in much better condition; the steeple stood tall; and many of the walls were still together. The stained-glass windows still stood in one piece and scattered the light on the ground in all sorts of colors. There were other people in the village, families and solitary travelers. They were all fairly thin, but they were clean and looked happy. Another picture showed, from a much higher point of view of an adult, a group of children playing together.

Surprise stopped the man's hand short from turning the page again; there she was. Considerably larger, healthier looking, and prancing among the children, was Bear. His little companion was mingling with the humans and taking part in their joy. Almost a child herself, but the size of a large dog.

A nostalgic sadness mixed with a sense of wonder filled the empty ribcage of the old man as he remembered with painful clarity, the lack of such an experience in his childhood. He had grown up surrounded by road-hardened adults in his travels, only living off necessity. There was never room for pets. The hard life he led wasn't kind to the tender disposition of a child.

From a young age, he had adapted to the solitude of the long walks. He remembered his own grandparents, a quiet old couple that had taken him on this journey long ago. His grandfather was a solemn man who laughed very few times but loudly when he did. His grandmother was a gentle soul; it was her that made light the weight of crushing loneliness to the child. Her good-natured smile was reflected in the expressions of the parents surrounding the playing children.

A genuine sweetness permeated from the photograph, evoking memories of her and the gentle protection she provided. This begged the question of what had happened to these families. The only thing that the old man knew for certain was that these people had likely made a long walk from civilization into the hungry wilds. The Traveler didn't know very much about the event that sparked the scattering of man, only the wars and desperate escape that followed. Only that people were there one day and gone the next.

Their possessions were untouched and left behind without a trace.

Normally, the next few pages would be reserved for other nights, but the wanderer flipped on to see what became of his little friend. The mystery unfolded as the photos showed less and less faces in the village; the smiles were gone from the faces that remained. On every page or so, there was a photo of a different family with their belongings packed. Perhaps they were merely moving on, the sad village and the surrounding flats didn't exactly spell bounty for a thriving community. Eventually, the old man's tanned finger turned the page to reveal nothing at all; the clear pockets meant to hold photos were empty and untouched.

This had been the cutoff point; the child had dropped her album and her teddy and off she had gone into the unknown. Her existence to the Traveler was snuffed out and every trace of that glimpse into her life with it. A suffocating and all too familiar sadness draped over the roof of the church that night. Inside, an old man lay mourning for a friend he never met. A small creature beside him grieving all she had ever known.

Looking at her now, the old man felt he finally understood her diminutive size compared to the past photos. He felt the loneliness shrinking him; all his strength ebbed away into thin air. The lost feeling that drove his heavy boot steps leagues away from sanctuary ever present in his empty ribcage.

That night, sleep came fitfully and feverish. The howling of the wind outside was his only lullaby. The screams infected his dreams into jumbled, flawed theaters that made no sense. The dusky hues of his dreams turned to a blinding light as cold as the winter outside. Sometimes he would wake with a start and question why he was in a rundown church in an abandoned town instead of his soft bed on the top of the mountain with his chickens clucking in the yard.

Sometimes he would wake not as a man, but as a frightened child on the fateful night of leaving home. He lost the ability to discern nightmare from reality and fought desperately to pick the better of the two. Whichever hurt less and would allow him to sleep. The confusion and desperation of his fevered mind turned the air sour. So the darkling hours passed painfully slowly until the sun-bleached everything a pasty gray through the clouds and snow. Fatigue and anxiety stole away his hunger and soaked his brow in a cold sweat, sickness clinging to his bones.

As the long years wore on and the Traveler aged, his natural strength wavered, and each shiver went deeper than before. The old man did not fear much, but sickness took from him so quickly what time was already leeching away. In times of illness, he could feel his vice-like grip on life slipping as he was pulled further into what lay beyond. When he woke from the nightmare, he couldn't quite wake. Bear hovered nervously watching as he let himself drift between consciousness and sleep. A new fragility had taken root and began to bloom in him, seemingly using his own life as sustenance like some sort of carnivorous flower.

He fought it, as fiercely as one can when illness reinvigorates and twists the imagination. His mind tried so desperately to find comfort, a peaceful respite to regain a footing. But that dusky room with the open window and the salty sea air coming through the curtains eluded him. His grandmother's perfume was all but unknown to him. Instead, he found himself back on the edges of the forest, engaged in terrifying eye contact with the ancient beast of the wood.

Instead of his stave and pack he had only a small lantern with weak, golden light. Those black hollow sockets bored into his eyes, peering past what any being should see into another. Always there to remind him of his place, or lack thereof. He belonged nowhere, as part of a past that held on so stubbornly, like a parasite. The earth and nature itself took back its domain save for whatever ground he stood upon.

His dream state took him on a tour through all of the things that he couldn't have. The old man wandered through this fog that illness had cast over his fevered eyes; his loneliness made material. He was alone in the world with no ties to the land or its creatures, yet he so obstinately and stubbornly remained.

He didn't truly wake until the sun had set and the room was dark and cold, as the fire had gone out with his neglect. Bear had curled into his side in a much easier slumber, her breaths pushing her ribs against him, the soft fur tickling slightly. The cold darkness beyond her realm of worry, she only had hers to worry about tonight. When the fever had gone, it left him still feeling cold and numb. He rose from the hammock to leave it swaying gently and stuffed more wood into the stove clumsily as if he still didn't have the full command of his fingers.

The dull red embers hissed and flecks of orange sprang upward as the heat found new fuel. Wearier than ever before, the Traveler held his hands out to the warmth. The light of the young flames illuminated his hands, and he looked at them as if for the first time. He thought of the depths of sickness when he rifted in between life and death, green and white. He thought of the loosening handle he had on his own lifeline; at his age, any illness could be his last.

And he still had so long to go before he could relinquish that grip. These thoughts ran rampant through his mind as he stared at the long spindly fingers and their large knuckles warped by time and pain. They were shaking slightly, having not yet regained their steady strength. To the old man it seemed that his own knurled hands were the last tie between him and his family. The echoes of his grandfather reverberated through the shape and size of his hands.

His grandfather was a stern man, not unkindly, but not nearly the merry person his wife was with her lavender perfume and ready smile. Although his features were blurred by time and warped by poor memory, the measure of his gaze and the shape of his hands remained with remarkable clarity. The way his practiced eye scanned the room, their deep brown color absorbing the little details, taking in everything. His hands were large and square, always clean. The palms were rough with callouses and tempered with experience; he never gripped too tightly nor dropped what he held.

In the Traveler's hands, he saw his own grandfather, the same shape and roughness in the palm. His fingers, however, remained distinctively his grandmother's with long bony fingers and oval nail beds. His were never going to be as elegant as hers; his nails were bitten and broken and dirty and his knuckles swollen with arthritis. There the old man sat, staring at his hands, remembering people.

Strangely, he felt better after recalling the people who kept him company for much of his journey. Their absence was felt, for sure, but all the more did he cling to their memory. How strange it was to him; he was alone in the world with no ties to the land or its creatures, yet he so obstinately and stubbornly remained.

He settled back into the hammock and let rest take him away. The slow sway of the hammock was reminiscent of summer breezes and the ripple of motion through young trees with their slender trunks of tender wood. It was a light sleep, but it was enough to chase the rest of the fever away from his threshold. The old man wouldn't remember what he dreamed of that night if he dreamed at all. But he welcomed the rising sun once more with the knowledge that, once more, he had endured.

He rose to face the day with the dreary hollowness that sleep deprivation leaves in its wake. Chores that would have only taken half a day took twice as long, but he was determined to do them. He changed his linens and clothes and took the extra time to rinse the sick from them. Despite how cold it made the room, he cracked the door ajar and flooded the room with fresh air from the plains when he went out to fetch some bones he had buried in the frozen snow for days such as this. When he was trapped, the cold would preserve the marrow inside and its healing nutrients.

A little shriek informed him of Bear's displeasure at being left behind. He burned the sage to cleanse the air once again, filling the room with the foul smell. But once he had finished and wearing his clean clothes and the walls were clean, he found he felt better. Fever to him almost seemed a being of its own, and it would stay if invited to, best to banish it before it could take root like a spore on a log. Before he knew it, dusk had descended on the sleeping ruins, and it was time to resettle for the night.

His fire was built up once again, and his little companion was nestled by his knees as he cooked their dinner. His appetite returned in full force. They feasted together on a mushroom and hare soup. The marrowbones gave a pleasing saltiness that radiated from their bellies to their limbs in satisfaction. His energy was slowly coming back into his muscles and his vision cleared once again. He reached for the weathered chapter book from his sack and resumed the adventures of young Marx, his sparrow, and the magic lantern holding his mother's precious soul.

The gigantic archway towered above the trees; its onyx stone was etched with mysterious carvings and embedded with sparkling jewels. The little boy Marx was awestruck at its majesty. More than that, he was curious about the mysterious creatures surrounding it. They were all mixed up; animals mixed with plants and had other parts of animals attached to them. They were big and small and all sorts of sizes in between.

More and more of these curious creatures were coming through the archway and into the clearing that surrounded the monolith. The boy hid in fear, for a few of these things had fangs to them. Being a clumsy child, he fell over a root and cried out as he went, and all the beasts scattered. A tense silence descended over the forest, and Marx emerged slowly from the tree he was hiding behind. The things had stopped coming through the arch, and the clearing was quiet.

The sparrow perched on his shoulder and hopped around nervously. The little boy ran around the structure on little legs to see what was on the other side. One side showed nothing special, just more trees and shrubs of the wood. The other side, however, showed nothing but black. This frightened the boy even further; the encroaching darkness showed nothing.

He held the lantern up to it to see if the magical rays could pierce the borders of obsidian light. The soft light did nothing to illuminate the mystery before him. But Marx was sure of his way forward, and being the eager little adventurer that he was, bravery was his way. And the child pressed onward into the darkness, not knowing where he was going, but hoping he would find what he was looking for.

After closing the book, the Traveler tucked it away again and began to run his hand gently over Bear's softback; he had taken quite a liking to pet the fine fur. When the animal didn't shy away from it, she remained fickle and moody about being pet. Sometimes her jaws would open and the cracked teeth would nip grumpily at his fingertips. That being said, today she welcomed the attention and continued her lazy half-slumber by his feet, her eyes hanging half-opened in a sightless survey. She only stirred when he placed her gently onto the hammock and set about making his tea.

More of the stinging nettle, a strong metallic smell, though not altogether unpleasant. He sipped it languidly as her black button eyes and those of the teddy looked at him pensively. The three just sat there, in that silence, save for the quiet sipping and splashing of drink. For a suspended moment, they were able to experience the absence of their loneliness.

In that brief minute, they were satisfied to just be, and be together. That night brought a more pleasant and restful sleep to our weary friend. He drifted in that same warm nothingness that true rest carries with it. His troubles were forgotten in a dark haze.

The next morning, something smelled different. There was no longer the icy staleness of deep winter. A new scent carried over the barren plains bleached by white snow and sun. He was outside gathering his firewood when it reached him. The old man closed his eyes and let the fresh wind fill his nostrils and swell his lungs, one thing came to mind. Green.

That omen of new life and kinder days. He had survived the winter yet again; neither the elements nor disease had caught up to him to halt his progress. Soon, he could resume his journey and reach the sea before the next snowfall. The closeness of his destination pushed triumph into his veins and reinvigorated his old aching limbs. His pains dulled and his burdens became lighter; his chores were done in what felt like a single bound. That day he decided to celebrate by going up to the frozen lake and catching a few small fish for him and his companion.

Obviously delighted by the fresh meat, Bear hung very close as he prepared the meal with her long nose twitching in anticipation. They feasted merrily that day, Bear not knowing why but considerably brightened at the better quality of food. The Traveler celebrated the approach of his destination and the answers that it no doubt held. He was so close to where he needed to be, where he had once felt the warm thing in his ribs spread happiness throughout his whole body.

The Traveler's newfound excitement seemed to make the time go by quickly. He could feel the winter receding and the wet, moist air of spring was coming. The color of nothingness gave way to earthen brown as the sun peeled away the white outer shell. His boots stuck in the mud stubbornly as he went about doing his business. Snow no longer fell from the heavens, instead the clouds were gray and weepy.

He attuned his hearing for the distant rolls of thunder and spent his early evenings watching bolts of electricity light up the sky. He admired the lightning and how it crawled across clouds and reached out with a jagged finger to touch the earth with a sharp crack. Fat tears of rain fell to the ground and steeped deep toward the sleeping seeds from the previous summer. *A couple of weeks of this*, the old man thought gingerly, *and the tiny seedlings would begin their sprouting*. The drowsy roots of the dead grasses would erupt anew from the ground and bathe the earth in waves of flaxen gold. His prophecy proved true as the sky warmed the earth quickly and life began to sprout again.

He went out more and more, enjoying the brief days of freedom from the confines of the room. Bear joined him often, perched happily on his shoulder. Her naps were now taken in the sweet fresh air, always taking her bear. One afternoon, she even allowed him to launder and somewhat restore the thing. Her eyes shifted nervously over his shoulder as he gently rinsed the matted fur from its cloth.

He hung it dry on an outside clothesline to air out the musty stench of neglect. The entire time Bear watched anxiously until the old man returned it to her smelling and looking like new. Or at least better. She was pleased with the improvement; it was almost like that was the final proof of goodwill that she needed. The budding trust between the two was in full bloom. United in survival.

As the days expanded in length and the wet mud dried. The Traveler knew it was about time to begin his journey once more. He then set about regathering his many bundles and dried goods to take his inventory. Everything packed and readied with his trademark neatness. However, among the items he had now to carry was a new burden.

What about his small, fragile companion? Compared to when the two first encountered each other, she had tripled in size in a seemingly unnatural phenomenon. She was up to his knee now and when she moved, her coat flashed a pearly iridescence on the surrounding terrain. That made her easily tracked by the hungry things that roamed the dark flatlands, and she was still very delicate looking. He worried after her ability to maintain walking for that long and having another being to protect put him at risk. Not once did she let go of the teddy and could still be seen carrying it gently in her jaws.

He glanced over to her, lying lazily on the hammock with the bear in her mouth. She met the Traveler's gaze with her dark intelligence, not quite understanding his intention. He then wondered how she would fare if he left her by herself once again to endure the sadness and barrenness of the great plains.

Blue

No one is more lost than one who loses themselves into the color blue. The hue is reserved for the deepest of oceans and widest of skies. At first, it's welcoming and bright; calming even, it lures you in to drink deep and look long. However, the endlessness of it swallows those feelings and before you know it, you are trapped in its atmosphere. Examples through literature and nature itself suggest that the bluer the thing is, the more hypnotic and dangerous its nature.

Sapphires, oceans, eyes: all things pull you in and never quite release. Curiosity lives in the color blue, and all its mysteries remain just beyond the reach of probing fingertips. The eternal abyss of shade beckons the lost one ever deeper into possible ruin.

With the bloom of spring came this peeking blue; the skies opened from the invasive whiteness into the freedom of periwinkle. The clouds were no longer dark and gray but as if fluffy bits of Bear's fur got lodged in the sky. The time for the adventure to resume was nigh. The old man had decided to embark the next morning right when the sun came up. The days were still a bit short, so he would drink in all the light he could.

Everything was packed and prepared save for the hammock. Each item was carefully folded and neatly tucked back into the canvas bag, now with a couple more patches than when the journey began. The book of Marx and his lantern wrapped, with a new affection, in a sweater to wick away any mildew. Bear watched him pack everything with a curiosity about her, the teddy hanging limply from her mouth. He tidied up the room with gratitude for his temporary home.

It was small and somewhat leaky, but it had sheltered him from the worst that the weather had to offer and kept him warm and safe within. It seemed as if there still remained a deity given to watch over that last refuge for its flock. The half-full photo album of the missing girl lovingly propped into the corner open, the images of her existence shown to the world once more. He settled in for the night to get his final night of rest before becoming a Traveler once more.

The man gazed about the cabin to rest eyes on the gentle creature sleeping soundly on the hammock in the corner they had shared together. A fondness toward her had taken refuge within the windy emptiness of the Traveler, standing bravely against the habits of solitude. He found that more than anything he felt a desperate need for her company. However voiceless she was, save for a few squeaks and whimpers, she filled the silence. Her nervous antics were even amusing at times, and despite his small meals, they filled him more having shared with someone.

He had come to depend on her just as much as she did him. Not unlike one swallowed in darkness but allowed a single candle. *If he changed the way he packed and left some things behind,* he thought, *perhaps he had room for her in his pack.* He made room at the top of his bag for her and lined it with a wool scarf just in case she caught the winds from the prairie. He would have to leave behind the book to conserve weight and space; if he wanted to bring his friend, he needed to bring only his necessities.

Hopefully, he could reach his destination before winter set in again. He stooped down and picked her up gently; she rolled over lazily. He chuckled softly at her enjoyment of allowing someone else to do the moving for her. He carefully tucked the delicate creature into the new nest of wool. A small pang of guilt gripped his belly as he looked at the teddy bear lying still tucked in. It would have to be left behind with their other comforts.

He picked it up and spent time inspecting it, only to set it lovingly in front of the album. That corner then became a memorial to the family that once lived in this sad place. A lasting testament to anything that would pass through, that there was once a time when smiles lightened up the walls and voices filled the empty air.

The town lay sadly watching the Traveler walk through it toward the western horizon. It would be empty once more, with nothing but ghosts and distorted time in its boundaries. The lake was still, only with the light breeze blowing tiny ripples over the surface. The buildings along the main dirt road were even more picked clean and broken down for the resources they could still offer him. Thin stalks of grass and reeds peaked from in between the sparse boarding.

It was then that the old man thought it truly dead. It seemed, quite literally, to be a skeleton of what used to be there, a monument of death and loss even. For all of its flaws and pathetic condition, the town had been his home and a hardy shelter during the rough months. Now even the lake had nothing more to gift to him. The fish would swim among its chilly waters and bite at the flies that lingered by the shore. The ground was dry now and gave softly underfoot as his boots took one step after another away from the heap of whitewashed rot.

After a while, when the town was nothing more than dots in the distance, the Traveler felt Bear stir in her sleeping spot on his back. He began to wonder about the reaction she would have to her new situation. Using her sharp, black nose, she peaked out from beneath the overlap of fabric. Seeing the empty world around her, she squawked in what seemed like shock and horror, and wriggled out of the pack to bolt. The Traveler reached out a rough hand and caught her, harder than he meant to, before she could leap off into the grasses, but she writhed furiously in his grip.

They struggled for a moment, him trying to pacify and calm her, and she trying to wrest away. With a surprising feat of strength, her little fangs sank deeply into the tanned flesh of his forearm, and he yelped in pain, surprising the both of them with the noise. The offended hand dropped her and off she went, back toward the tiny buildings in the distance, reduced to a streak of white against all the yellow. His stomach heavy with feelings of betrayal and shock, his legs moved almost on their own to pursue the creature. She outran him, much to his baleful frustration, but he was determined to keep her in his line of sight.

By the time he arrived back within the confines of the village, he could only walk and just glimpsed her tail vanishing into the door of the church. He knew what she would be looking for; he could feel it in his gut and was proven correct when he arrived back within the confines of the room. Huddled back in the corner with her bear, almost a mirror reflection of when he first saw her. Hanging onto it with the same fierceness that she always did; only this time, it was not fear but fury that hissed like steam from her jaws. She glared at him with a new suspicion in her obsidian eyes.

Warm blood dripped down his hand and dripped shiny red onto the bleached floorboards as he knelt slowly by her corner and measured her stance carefully. He hadn't seen her like this since winter first began and despaired at how quickly her nature had reverted back to feral suspicion. He offered up his uninjured hand to her and watched her sniff it cautiously, almost as if a stranger. She didn't let him any closer than that; the quiet snap of her jaws showed his blood still clinging wetly to the dark fur.

The fragile trust between them was broken, almost as if it never existed to begin with. His attempt to take her away from this monument of mourning was beyond what she could do. He receded to the opposing corner and sank heavily to the ground, he still held onto the hope that she would rally, and the shock would pass.

The Traveler desperately waited for that amity to return and for his friend to join him in the journey forward to stave off the solitude that had been his only companion for decades. He knew it was selfish and desperate, but still, he remained. Neither moved for what seemed like eons but, in reality, was no more than an hour. It never did; the warmth that emanated from the creature was gone and a feral hostility had taken residence. It donned slowly upon him that he had lost this battle of wills.

He felt the wind in his ribs, more so now than ever, as he picked up the things that he had left behind to make room for her. The book went back into the top of the bag to take up the space she never would. Those beady black eyes watched his every move as he replaced the straps over his shoulders and set off again without her. His steps even heavier this time, he exited the raddled town once again. The quiet crunching of grass behind him told him that his wintertime companion was following him.

A tiny flicker of hope lit within him, only to be snuffed out when he flicked his eyes back to see her. Somehow, she had grown even larger; she stood a full head above him. Her fangs now long and glossy and corded muscles rippled under a pearl-like, glowing coat. She still carried the teddy with the care he had come to know her by. Fresh, newfound terror ripped his eyes away from her and seemed to carry him to his exit from her territory.

Only when they arrived at the border did the old man dare to look back at her a second time. She sat there at the edge and returned his gaze, towering over the broken-down remains of the village. Her image reflected the stillness surrounding her. For a moment, they stayed there, staring at each other in a swollen silence.

He longingly searched for the fragile creature he knew, who had needed his kindness and care to thrive. She saw a trespasser fleeing from her territory. This time, the Traveler recognized, in her dark eyes, the will of the giant Elk God he had met in the forest. In that same moment, he came to truly comprehend what the thing standing before him was.

However small and weak that creature had appeared, she was the one given watch over this small patch of earth. Some time ago; after humanity had all but vanished, she rose with the rest of the ancient strangers to walk the ground again. It was she who had allowed sanctuary to visiting travelers and accepted the tributes they gave her in repayment. When they were gone from the earth, she had shrunk in her despair until the last, pathetic wisp of humanity stumbled upon her ruins. The dying sentiment had allowed him to stay within her boundaries out of remaining goodwill toward the human race.

She accepted what he gave her and took watch over him as her last worshiper, her final adorer. Now, she was warning him again that he did not belong here; he was a visitor and a trespasser, nothing more. Now, he could never return. So, there he left her to forever linger in-between the walls of an extinct past. She would stand there forever to remind all who passed through of the unending white that lies at the end of all things.

Her relentless clinging to what was lost was what defined her existence now. Taking an Old God, however small she might have once been, was out of the question. He remembered the little shrine to the memories of the little lost child. In a way he, through that small insignificant action, had enforced the illusion that she was so frantically hanging onto.

The teddy was her final gift that he had taken away, something from a child to ingratiate the unknown architects of the end of humanity. And now all that was left of the god's terrain was a broken-down reminder of what was lost. The Traveler could not help but think of the wretchedness of such an existence. One for the past and pined for the things that will never return to you. To be forever defined by your own loss and forgo the way forward to perpetual stillness in those lost moments. She lived in the past, but existed in the now, and those who refuse to either breath or perish are doomed to forever be placeless. It was with those thoughts that he left her to the monument of her grief, the long walk alone resumed once more.

The Woods

The Traveler dared not look back until he was sure that he was out of sight from the village before he glanced in that direction. He was wrestling with the anger of being expelled, the betrayal of the bite, which still stung, and the simple sadness of Bear's fate. When he did care to glance over his shoulder, the collection of buildings had been eaten up by the flat horizon. He was truly alone again. Hours passed slowly with only the soft crackling of dry grasses beneath his boots to mark the passage of time. One crunch per second. He didn't care to note the hours or the minutes, but clung to the reliable pacing to carry him far away. Hours later the light began to die again. Despite it being spring, the nights would still cast over a chill that stung the air coming into his lungs.

It felt like the cold somehow crystallized within his chest and throat to give them a dull ache. That night, he brought out the canvas previously used as his hammock in the church and propped it back into its original state as a tent. There was plenty of dead wood around that would make ample fuel for a fire to keep the invading shadows away. He still read by firelight from the story of little Marx. The flickering somehow added to the mystery that unfolded from its pages. Hearing the familiar tale brought him a measure of comfort in his fresh loss.

The story picked up after Marx had gone through the giant obsidian archway in the center of the forest.

The child found himself in a dank, stone room lit only by some old candles. It was quiet and warm, which brought him a tiny bit of comfort. The sparrow spun in the air and chirped her dismay at the new surroundings. Nonetheless, the fine strands of glowing red hair led down a dark corridor.

Raising the lantern above his little head, he took off following it. His footsteps echoed off of the moldy walls. The glowing hair led him to a staircase, it winded upward in a spiral. Already winded from his overexcited running, Marx took his time going up the stairs. They seemed to go on forever until the boy came upon what felt like a closed window. Desperate for light he pushed the shutters open to reveal the very forest he had just left.

He even saw the archway in the distance. But he didn't think he had gone that far, nor did he see a tower like the one he was in. Judging by how high above the treetops he was, he was in a building far taller than anything from his hometown. He knew he still had a long way to go, so he kept running up the stairs with his short, stubby legs, with determined little tapping sounds.

After what seemed like forever, the stairs finally turned into a flat hallway. It led to a heavy oak door that the boy had to throw his whole body weight against to pry open. It gave way and the boy tumbled into a library the likes of which he had never seen.

It was now that the Traveler saw what his grandfather saw within the pages of the book. A fable that reflected the happenings of the real world. The old man fancied himself on a similar adventure to the boy, trying to reclaim that which was lost to them, he could imagine his grandfather's own burdens feeling lighter with the feeling of a kindred spirit. He likely felt a bright kinship with the child that brought a much-needed lift in his spirits. When the same calamity befalling humanity happened to his wife, he delved even deeper into the story. Having a companion, fictional or otherwise, probably illuminated his vision with the possibility of other perspectives. It was then that he could move forward and embrace the unknown fate that awaited him.

The Traveler laid his back on the ground and gazed up into the night sky full of stars. *His own fate was beyond what he could see,* he thought to himself, and half wondered, and half hoped if he could meet his own with the same peace. At the very least, he knew he was leaving no one else behind, whether death or something else took him. Though he couldn't decide if this was a boon or a burden.

The Traveler had such limited encounters with other people as a child that the concept was almost alien to him. And that made it alluring, oftentimes when he found himself very aware of his solitude he would allow himself the hypothetical. When his mind wandered in this way, he enjoyed walking through his world, taking in the sights of nature, and pondering what another person might say or think about them. He liked to think that he would enjoy the intercourse of conversation. Something he always saw his grandparents do; they put their foreheads together and spoke in whispered tones.

Their expressions were inquisitive and assured almost at the same time. At that moment, he thought they were the only two people in the world. Their intimacy shown through in such a delicate manner. They would create ideas and plans all their own when they pushed their heads together like that. Through the eyes of their small grandson, it seemed that all of the world's problems could be solved by simply joining in intimate conversation. It was from that moment on that he would harbor a secret jealousy and yearning for the closeness that would lead to such an interaction.

There were many things that the Traveler would like to have spoken aloud to someone who could listen. There is a distinct difference between speaking to oneself and speaking to someone with the faculties to listen and offer up a graceful reciprocation. The most of which consisted of his inner thoughts on the workings of nature. He found great peace and amusement in the goings-on around him as the sleepy world woke up to embrace the warmth of spring. He wanted to share his distaste of picking flowers; something he had seen his grandmother do often before the great pilgrimage.

He didn't like how they withered so sadly despite being placed carefully in water. Normally, hardy blooms rendered almost determined to die an ugly, slow death that putrefied the water they were put in. As he grew, he realized that picking them, the act of tearing them from the soil they were born from, was done with the full knowledge that their ugliness was inevitable. He couldn't decide fully whether or not that was intentionally cruel or that all the flowers were good for. He remembered asking his gentle grandmother why she liked to pluck the prettiest flowers to watch them die, and the curious stare he earned in reply.

She didn't speak words in return, but never again did he see her snipping the stems of flowers to put in vases. As an adult, he thought of this often, especially when the world around him bloomed in abundance and thrived for weeks in their warm soil. He remembered the brevity of the life they lived entrapped within glass vases and how soon their sweet fragrance turned to rotten stink and the clear water turned rancid. If he were torn so suddenly from the ground, he would then ask himself, would he then want to blossom and bless the one that displaced him? These thoughts sat idly in his brain and, in the absence of someone to share them with, were blown away by the spring wind.

So passed the week of travel before the foliage began to change, as there was now foliage rather than just grasses. What started as dry bushes and dust now sprouted trunks and shot upward toward the clouds. The plains had turned into woodlands once more. The Traveler was grateful for the overshadowing of branches and leaves before the harshness of the summer sun could further bake the wrinkled skin off of his nose and forehead. They were already a chapped red that stung as he touched it.

A stream crossed his path, and he knelt by it to drink from the cool water. His reflection stared blankly at him, a tired-looking man as bleached by the sun as the wide prairie he had just left. His gray hair was white now, touched by time, and he had new wrinkles to add to the forest of lines on his face. His browned skin tinted pink with fresh sunburn. The Traveler dunked his head into the rushing waters and let it calm the fevered skin. The cold revived him a bit so that he could continue forward into the underbrush.

He decided that he would camp out in a small thicket for a while to restock. His reserves were as sad as they had ever been. His stomach gnawed itself in hunger. That night he ate the last of his dried meat and mushrooms. The acorn flour was gone completely long ago, so there was no more bread to be had.

When the sun rose to greet the next morning in peach and gold, he woke easily and set about creating his traps. The stream nearby would at the very least provide fresh water if not fish. With spring came the sprouting of young herbs and vegetables perfect for picking. He found more dandelion leaves and wild garlic. The soft tenderness of the plants crushed under his teeth as he ate to pass the time.

His hunger was abated slightly; the gnawing alleviated. The trek was enjoyable; since he was staying in the area, he was able to take his time and drink deep from the new world. If a herd of deer crossed his path, he had the time to sit and stare at their peaceful grazing. There was a whole host of new birds to admire as well as fresh views to see. His search continued at an unrushed pace until he had once again filled his little sack with bounty.

The next two weeks passed in relative comfort as the sun pierced through the leaves to dapple the ground in light and warmed the dirt. The forest was stained a yellow-green, not unlike the broken shards of stained glass on the floor of the old church he had left behind. The traps caught small prey that he dispatched as quickly and mercifully as he could and set their carcasses up in the smoking shelter he made once again. Pelts began lining the campsite, and he set about stitching them together to add to his threadbare coat. His hands were large and rough, but he had skill with a needle.

He stitched together a new collar and cuffs. He pieced a new blanket together and would roll it out on the forest floor to cushion his old bones for sleep. It was comfortable, and he found that he slept better each night spent on the soft furs. They were warm enough to even sleep on without other blankets. Nightly he laid on the new pad and read from the yellowed pages of his book and delved once more into Marx's life and adventures.

The library towered over the boy's head. A huge spiral staircase swirled around the edges of the walls and up it he climbed. The building was quiet and smelled of paper; his sparrow leaped off his shoulder and flew around happily. Windows lined the tall tower and let the sunlight in. Going up the staircase seemed to take hours, but eventually, he reached the top.

There he saw the most curious of sights; the top of the tower was not a library but a lighthouse surrounded by windows. The glass revealed that he was not surrounded by forest but by the beach. Ocean spread widely around him, and there wasn't a tree in sight, just black sand and gray water. At this point, the boy found himself greatly distressed by the strangeness of the place. He hugged the magical lantern to him as tears trickled down his face. So he sat there, a sad young boy alone in the world and in a strange place. Surrounded by strange things.

It saddened the old man to see his young friend, no matter how fictional, in such a state. In his much older eyes, children ought to be shielded from such misfortune at all costs. Over the course of his travels, he didn't see many other children, but those he did meet had seen too much, and too early. He held back the desire to read on and discover how the book would end, but his eyelids were heavy, and there was nil he could do to slow their descent down his eyes. Worry melted away from him like snow from a branch as he let himself slip away into sleep.

Once his trapping was completed and his stocks restored, a newly rejuvenated Traveler trekked through the woods and camped alongside the stream, now a larger river, each night. Its friendly bubbling was a welcome noise to break up the disembodied sounds of night. It was strange, this part of the woods. He had not often been in a forest this temperamental. There was a particularly dense fog that hovered over the ground and smothered anything in sight.

Only his keen hearing, trained over decades to seek signs of danger, guided the old man forward. Following his woodland guide of running water, he made quite a distance without alarm. It didn't recede until nightfall and the earth became bathed with cold moonlight; the forest showing its deeper, more malicious side. Blue chased the bright, happy colors of the day into submission and wove its magic into the plants and animals of the forest. These new creatures of darkness chirped and howled into the free rein from the domineering sun. At least, the Traveler thought to himself, that it was only at night.

He was uneasy in this forest; unlike the mountain stag's domain where everything was silent and growing, there was a wilder hunger here that bragged of a salacious appetite. The old man was reminded daily of his dark times on the plains with dreams full of prowling sea creatures feasting on the corpse of a sunken whale. He found himself praying for the sun to come back and drive these darklings away, only to wake to yet more of the milky-shrouded sky. It was after the third or fourth day of walking through this muck, that the old man began to notice signs that even now he was not alone, even in the daytime.

A new, animal smell lingered in the air. Something musky and wet, like damp hair and dirty nails. And there were times he swore that he could hear an ambiance of snapping twigs and scraping claws in the undergrowth. He was used to that at this point and had originally thought it as nothing more than a stray herd of deer that journeyed alongside him. However, these sounds persisted and drew closer with each passing sunrise.

As time passed into the afternoon of his tenth day into the strange woods, the Traveler came to understand his situation. He knew that he was being stalked by a band of hunters that didn't take kindly to his presence. They warned him with their sounds, be it the rustle of their disturbance of the landscape, or by the whines and chitters of their barks, if they could even count as barks. Judging by the terrifying sounds he heard, be it day or night, he counted ten or twelve of them. More than he could scare off. This fed a growing pit of fear in his belly that lurched heavily with each new cry.

He took to carving a sharp point into the tip of his trusty stave. He had been working on Bear's resemblance standing tall and powerful above the skyline of the town, but now he focused on harrowing an edge to a tool of exploration into a weapon. It wouldn't keep away all of them, but it might mean the difference between reaching his destination alive or tumbling into an early, muddy grave. The eyes circled him in the abyss and taunted at his work during these nights spent close by the fire. Still, onward he pressed, always harassed by the Pack and the dread that consumed him slowly.

At night, the old man would pile his fire high with as much damp fuel as he could find so that when sunset came and dusk ruled, he at least had some defense against the encroaching eyes. They pierced from the darkness like golden sparks that threatened to snap at any fragment of clothing or body part that strayed too far from the light. They got closer each night and barked and whined as if to keep him up on purpose. One day, when the air hung particularly thick and damp and his eyes peeled against the fog, he caught a glance at what was following him in those woods.

He didn't spy much, but what he was able to carve from the veil of murky white, froze him solid inside. In his own mind, he gifted them a name as terrible as they appeared, as he had done so with all the strange beings in his path so far.

The Pack.

The Pack

Because of this strange fog that cloaked everything in its white haze, the Traveler couldn't see much other than the way forward. His heading, at the start of his journey, was always west toward the setting sun, in the hopes of hitting a coastline eventually. His trek through the forest led him into a particularly old part of it; the trees stood impossibly tall and thick among twisted roots the width of his wingspan. His breathing became labored not just because of the effort gone to climbing over those roots but also the thickness of the muggy air. He breathed hard in the humidity, the water in the air almost half drowning him. His rush and growing panic gave him no reprieve.

The water in the mud exhausted him. Silhouettes of broken, rotting trunks sticking sideways from the ground set his mind quite ill at ease due to their resemblance to what his imagination told him was following him. Green vines and moss covered the corpses of fallen trees like a gigantic green spider had laid her web over everything. The earth laid out mottled and misshapen like a poorly healed scar.

He was working his way up an unnaturally steep hill covered in slippery mud when something caught the toe of his boot and brought him crashing into the mushy ground.

The wet earth clung to his aching limbs and water seeped into his clothes. The weight of his pack and clothes suddenly too waterlogged for him to lift. He was stuck there. Rendered helpless as a fly caught in the sticky lace web of a spider.

He struggled to find his bearings; his frenzied panic tinted his vision red. He was certain that his faltered movement would alert the Pack to his folly and weakened state, and they would descend. The thought of their gnashing teeth and their dirty wet animal smell closing in were all he could think about. His breathing began to come out in rasps as he determinedly pushed himself upright again. His pack was lopsided and only hanging on by a strap, but he hoisted his weight back into balance by grasping one of the towering roots nearby.

He looked around frantically, trying desperately to see the threat. But he was alone. The forest was suspended in a stillness, and there were no signs of the creatures. His blood still pounded in his ears with alarm. Marking the seconds ticking by with each thump.

His sight twitched toward every direction to spy a hint of movement, only to see nothing. In embarrassed and panicked fury, his eyes glared at what had tripped him. What he saw made him as still and silent as the sleeping wood around him.

Laid out before his widened eyes was an ancient metal graveyard. He had seen one before, only fresher, and not quite as grown over with leaves and rust. Long ago, he remembered, before humanity began disappearing into thin air. There was a long war fought by equally forgotten sides, at least by the old man who had been not much more than a child then. All he knew now was that the majority of either side didn't know why they barraged each other in a storm of metal and fire.

The result of which were vicious scars left on not just the people, but the earth as well. Thus, was the soft ground around him stained red with jagged, rusty bits of shrapnel littering the forest floor. The red dust stood out boldly against the green undergrowth. Bits of the encompassing white fog draped lazily over the old ruins of battle, looking like a poorly wrapped bandage upon the wounded earth. It was then that the old man realized the silence that drenched the air; there were no longer snaps and rustles that signified the Pack's movement. Instead, they stood motionless, surrounding him on all sides, fully unveiled from their shroud of mist, and boring into him with sharp yellow eyes.

Their appearances were strange; their outlines hunched over and crippled-looking, but ferocious. What should have been stocky, muscle-bound limbs of Wolven origin seemed more fragile and lankier. Definitely canine, but there was a delicacy in their joints that didn't match the still-long claws that protruded from them. *Almost a rabbit-like litheness*, the Traveler thought, *they stood at the border between predator and prey*. From their haunches sprouted red-capped growths of fungal character in that otherworldly blur of flora and fauna that permeated through all the world's terrible new creatures.

Also sticking out painfully from their flesh were bits of rusted, broken metal. They matched the scenery in the most desolate, heart-breaking way. It was then that it finally dawned on the old man the magnitude of the place he was standing. This was their grave and their birthplace; they had slumbered through gunfire and bombs but had risen with the accompanied scars left behind. Instead of being graceful like bounding rabbits and powerful like a family of wolves, their movements were limp and broken.

The reminder of man's folly embedded deep into their flesh to fester and weaken them. There were seven of them standing before the Traveler, looking forlorn and hungry. From their darkly golden, hollow eyes he knew, again, that same feeling of being an unwelcome trespasser. In all the places he had been before, the other beings didn't have a reason to hate him until he transgressed in some way. These dogs, for starving wild dogs they most resembled, acted out of half-maddened fear. He saw the pain that they felt, and knew humanity was responsible for it. And he was painfully aware of what they now demanded, a grievous penance.

With tense slowness, the Traveler raised his stave before him in anticipation, the glossy wood cool and solid in his hands. Despite their emaciated and jagged appearances, they had numbers and teeth on their side. He brandished his makeshift spear in a show of fearlessness, nothing but empty smoke, as his knees were almost collapsing beneath him in terror. They all stared at each other tensely; the Pack began moving closer slowly with their heads down low and lips peeled back to bear rows of yellowed, malformed teeth. Panic began to breathe life through the Traveler's veins as he waved the long wooden stave over his head in desperation.

He cried out in a feral roar in an attempt to scare them away. His hoarse voice cracked and weary from disuse, but his fury came through. It did the job, and the Pack hesitated in uneasy anticipation.

As quickly and carefully as he dared, the Traveler walked backward down the hill. His steps were still achingly slow, but no longer burdened with the attempt at stealth. Still brandishing his staff threateningly at the creatures, his back to the trees and his eyes focused on the Pack as they followed him. The creatures were hauntingly steady with their hungry glare at him. They never took their eyes from his. As they advanced, he noticed their odd limps and how the fractured edges of metal made them move clumsily and painfully. *They are just as mangled as they look*, he thought hopefully.

At this observation, a new opportunity revealed itself to him. His thoughts darted around his skull with rushed, sloppy calculations to determine how close he was to the sound of a river behind him, and how quickly he could reach it. Then, with a quicker shuffle, he changed direction toward the riverbank. The Pack followed; their glaring eyes now darting from his feet, to his eyes, then to his weapon. They weren't quite realizing his goal, but not liking that he was moving away from them.

A few of them began to growl and snap with a click of their jaws at him, closing the distance between them. Once he was within a stone's throw from the river's edge, the old man dove into the shallows. The frigid waters stole his breath away with their icy currents. There were still glass-like shards of fragile ice drifting lazily along the surface. The cold sent him into a shock, and his head dipped beneath the surface. His face stung horribly from being drained of heat and life. He fought to regain control of his limbs as the river swept him away, but the culmination of fear, shock, and desperation returned to him, briefly, the litheness of youth.

In a burst of energy, he broke through the freezing water and gulped the air with a shuddering gasp. He only needed to fight to stay afloat with his weight and belongings. The current was spiriting him away from his pursuers. In a painful lurch, his body collided with a dead tree and he gripped the dead wood with a strength only the desperate have access to.

His apparent escape infuriated the Pack, and they lurched along the shore and howled their displeasure. A few of them did wade in after him but flinched away in agony as the cold waters made contact with the shrapnel in their hides.

The Traveler, with his years of weathered journeying, had figured that the creatures lived with their injuries for quite some time. If these were from the same war that the old man recalled, then that would likely have been half a century or more of cycling winters and wet springs. These wounds were old and putrefying slowly. No creature in such condition could fight the monstrous pull of the water. But it seemed that he had been mistaken; a few of them delved into the water to pursue him. No sooner did their slender bodies enter the water than they began to shriek and struggle; their limbs disobeying them with injury and weakness. One did make it onto a lone rock standing against the current and slumped pathetically against the black stone.

The old man took a moment to take in the creature as it lay whimpering; fresh blood oozing out of the shell in its shoulder. The cold would seep through the wounds and a red dust would infect its blood, and it would wither and madden if it did not succumb to fatigue and cold first. Either way, he was getting away in one piece this time. An early fate avoided. His gamble had paid off and the creatures didn't dare to follow him deeper into the water. Instead, they glowered at him from the rocks and howled to their discontent. The horrible sounds like a distorted song of hunger and cold, hardship incarnate.

With the immediate threat avoided, the old man now had to face the dangers of his faltering swimming. Adrenaline had given him a temporary invincibility that now left him in the throes of fatigue. The currents of the river's flow wrested him from the branch he clung to and swept him away toward the South. The weight of his clothes and pack had drunk heavily from the dark waters and began to drag him down. He struggled furiously as he sank.

He grasped blindly in the water in a desperate search for something to grab as the water rushed over his face and into his mouth and nose. He inhaled in an onslaught of dirty wet that had him sputtering and he willed himself not to gasp; his lungs burned with the effort. Something sharp and cold sliced across his hand, flaying the skin open. He remained in the grips of panic, so there was a numbness that blocked the worst of the pain. He reached out once more and grasped hard stone, not caring how much more it pierced his slippery skin.

That little bit of anchorage let him peek his head above the surface and see what he had clung to, it was a large flat rock that hovered just above the rapids. In his last bit of strength, he hoisted himself onto it and out of the water. There he lay, panting heavily as his energy left him like the body heat he lost by the second. He held up his right hand

and watched tiredly as bright blood dribbled out of his flesh. The pain was coming to him in waves, it radiated up his arm and to his brain to dull his thoughts like a drug.

In his stupor, he lingered there, fascinated by the fluid that fueled his body spill out of him and leaving him that much colder. He brought up his other hand and examined the scar that Bear had left him in her escape. It was pale and white compared to the tan of his skin, a little streak of death on his flesh. He gazed again at the red blood on his right hand, the dribble now an ooze as the cold squeezed his veins shut to slow loss of blood.

A blurry thought came to him as he lay there, made stupid by the pain, the colors of rust and death on his hands as if he held them. As if he dealt them out wherever he went. Perhaps in the eyes of the wounded and sick Pack, he had.

Eventually, his trance was broken by the distant screams of the Pack on the opposing bank, and he set to work staunching the rest of the bleeding. A wet rag had to do. He wound it tightly around his wide, square palm. The wetness of the bandage diluted the blood running through it to delicate strings of crimson. With slow, labored steps and huffing as he went, the Traveler trudged from stone to stone, away from the center of the river and to the other side.

Looking up, he saw the blue of the sky tinting to peach as the sun began his descent into his indigo bed. He had to make fire and dry everything before the early spring air robbed him of the little warmth that the water and blood loss had left behind. He bundled together twigs, leaves, and dry branches as he went. Whatever dry articles he could find, at least; the fog had drenched everything in moisture. As he gathered desperately, he looked about him for a natural shelter. Something to take the brunt of the wind that he wouldn't have to erect.

There was a rock fixture nearby that he thought looked promising. The trek there was heavy and slow, with his wet boots sloshing in the mud and his socks squelching uncomfortably inside them. But once he arrived, he let everything clinging to his shoulders drop with a wet-sounding slap. It wasn't much, but the rock was solid, and most of the windchill was blocked. In terms of how his day had begun, he was making promising progress.

The Traveler rushed to make a fire, his hands were unsteady and he shivered horribly. The wet wood struggled to light and when it finally did, it spat angrily at him and the smoke was milky white and pungent. He piled it high with the sticks he had gathered and laid out his possessions on the ground to dry in the heat. A knot tied in his gut as he warily took measure of what the water had taken from him. What food had been spoiled, and would his carefully packed medicines be ruined. The pit in his stomach formed by dread dropped further down, almost to his feet, as he picked up the sweater that protected the book. It was soaked through; the fibers of what was normally a navy-blue sweater were inky black with moisture. It smelled already of mildew and rot.

Worry buzzed in circles around the old man like a fly to a carcass as he unwrapped the soggy sweater that encased the precious story of Marx and his magical lamp. Upon revealing the book, he saw that it was ruined. The pages, already decayed by time and use, slipped off in clumps of ruined paper. His last treasure to remember a simpler time, his last kindred spirit, was gone. To be sure that he couldn't save at least the last chapter, he pried open the cover and was greeted with a soppy mess of yellowed tan. The ink through which flowed the legend of a little boy finding his way in the world had spread into an incoherent blur.

The only one that would read to the end of the book was the riverbed and the bottom feeders. For all their failure to take his life, he felt that the Pack had exacted its revenge and made him drink deeply from their bitter cup. It was then that the Traveler felt the full extent of his own sorrow. Something about losing this one last comfort opened some floodgate that he was previously ignorant to.

How curious it is to lose one thing and be reminded of everything else you have lost. You take a tally of all that is taken from you but don't truly look at it until the last ball has dropped. Then, placed before you in horrible, devastating detail is a list of everything you've lost. The Traveler was no different; he saw this list of his, and it was years long and full of not just things, but people as well. The old man sat back and let the memories drown him in his own uncried tears.

His chickens; the gentle, merry birds, that bickered incessantly for his attention. That tiny little cottage on the top of a mountain withstood the harshest tundra gales for decades and kept him safe and warm inside. His little companion, Bear, who had made him work so hard to earn her trust only to reject him and set him on his lonely way. Leaving her in that miserable, dead place. The hands that guided his from childhood into youth, only to slip away before his journey's end. The smell of lavender and rustle of paper; a boisterous laugh and steady guidance. The sharing of intimate conversations and stories within a family all his own. In that moment, the old man sat back on his heels and wept to the ink-stained sky. For it was now that he had no choice but to acknowledge that he didn't belong anywhere, and that his time was lost.

It is a heavy feeling: loss. To lose something that you hold dear tinges the light that you see everything else through an orange-yellow color of fearful anger. Through its eyes, you see the things you love as so breakable and as if they are hovering over a precipice, about to fall in. From this is born an anxiety and insecurity that feeds with each new loss. It demands more greedily until it swallows you up in its endless hunger.

The old man sat there under the stars and let them blink cruelly at him for what seemed like a long time. They, who were never alone in the sky, seemed to twinkle in mocking condescension that only eternal bodies do.

When he regained at least some of his senses again from his reverie, he was able to search his thoughts for comfort. He thought back to the gentle, wizened advice his grandmother shared with him in the midst of any chaos. She said this when they passed some fallen settlement or spied the abandoned belongings of another pilgrim lost to everything. According to her, some fell into the hopeless despair of the ruins around them and drifted away into nothing, he heard her voice more clearly than ever before as he welcomed this memory,

"Into the Wild Blue," as she said.

It was this sentiment that flooded the Traveler's lungs when he most wanted to scream out his frustration. A nagging question that asked of him which he would be. Was he destined to succumb to oblivion and fade away, or if his wounds would fester and he would plunge into fever, clinging rabidly to survival? His own grief swallowed his voice and asked him cruelly who would answer his calls for help, for advice on what he would do. Any ties of his to the place he belonged were gone now. He was only a wanderer with a supposed destination that most likely was nothing more than a crater or skeleton fashioned from empty planks.

He was a relic, a stubborn remainder of a closed era. He had been born to a world that denied him. He knew it, the Old Gods knew it, the dark and hungry grief knew it. It would be easy, a kindness even, to let the breeze carry him away and leave his tired, old body behind to rot slowly and feed the grasses and fungi. The old man felt himself falling into that precipice that his kind had given themselves to, himself perhaps the most fragile of them all. He sat in his desperation and stared blankly at the beautiful, cruel stars above him; giving in and waiting for finality.

That is until the wind changed once again.

The Path

The rocky place the Traveler had taken refuge in was well-fortified; not quite a cave, but a structure that had him protected on three sides and left him open to the western sky. Until then, the Traveler was sheltered from the wind that was coming in from the north. As he knelt there, a new breeze bathed him in a familiar, salty scent. What used to be a hint now was a pungent aroma; it had never before been so strong and close. The smell of home filled his nostrils and bathed his lungs, and the chill coming off the sea raised bumps through his skin. Then, just as he needed it most, he remembered more clearly than ever before, his destination.

The place he had come from was a small town perched along a rocky cliff that overlooked the ocean. He recalled, faintly, his neighborhood being a collection of tiny pastel cottages with white picket fences. There was a gate that always creaked when it swung open; his young ears could always tell when someone came and went throughout the day. His grandmother loved lavender and grew it in the backyard so she could spend her early mornings surrounded by the sharp herbal scent. The walls of the home were decorated with ceramic insects that held dried blossoms. They brought good luck and warded away sickness.

His grandfather worked with wood, always smelling of earthy varnish and constantly brushing shavings from his hair and clothing. In the backyard, surrounded by the purple blooms, was a clean, whitewashed workshop. Out of this came wonders both large and small, but all made of silky, polished wood. Their two worlds collided and merged to mix wood, oil, and flowers; a feast of sights and smells. They walked together along the cliff's edge to look at the paintings in the sky, and tell tales of things that never happened. Sometimes, if he was feeling brave, the Traveler would peek his small head over the edge to look at the black sand beaches below. The rock and sand stood firmly against the rolling mass of the ocean, and storms churned the waters black; they seemed to pull wandering eyes in with their treacherous dance.

The sound of the waves crashing rang in his ears as he came back to himself after this vision. His ribcage was still inhabited by the gnawing emptiness that had defined his pilgrimage, but he slept deeply that night. His dreams were cradling him, rather than haunting him; granting the elder reprieve from his misery for the night.

When the sun came up once more and shed golden locks across the landscape, the Traveler woke to find his clothing acceptably dry and his wounded hand aching. With great care, he peeled back the cloth to see the damage in the morning light. The stone from the river had ripped a wide gash across his palm. In a morbid curiosity fueled by his own damaged flesh, he held his hand up to the light.

The bleeding had stopped, but the damage was done. A sliver of sinew and muscle showed through the gash and stared back at him as if he had cut an eye open on his own hand. Strangely pale compared to the vibrant red that had flowed from it earlier, the skin was painfully swollen and tight around the edges of the crevasse. *At least the bleeding stopped*, he thought, and collected his bone needle from his surviving supplies. While his medicines were either destroyed or swept away, he had some surviving thread that he kept for such emergencies. There was a time where an ill-placed ax or a particularly adventurous fox caused him to need to stitch himself together. The process was slow and painful, and the old man wrapped his handiwork in a dry bandage and hoped that it wouldn't fester.

With the light of a new day came a wary optimism as the old man looked over his provisions again. Although his various medications and most of the dried food he had were gone or too soaked to prove any use, he still had the means to forage and trap. Dirty water had rendered his pack disgusting with a fetid smell from the wet fabric. The jerky he made was still good but would need to be eaten quickly before it had a chance to rehydrate and rot.

He sighed and resigned himself to the tidying up of what he could take with him. The feeling of dry clothes on his skin lent him a pitiable amount of comfort. Once he had eaten what he had and repacked what else remained, his burdens sat easier on his back. Whether it was from the reduced weight of lost items or from the release of his wild emotions into the wind the night before, he didn't bother to distinguish. At any cost, he was grateful for the lightened load on his spine that still ached from sleeping in cold rock.

Holding the ruined book in his hands, its pages now dry but warped into a wordless mess by the water, the Traveler walked back to the river he came from. It had been both his savior and the thief who made off with his most precious things. He spent what felt like a long time hesitating at the edge, but with a resolute arm, he threw the story into its dark, wet grave. Its words then lost to the ages in the murky depths. The river had taken from him the story, now she could have the rest of the book, to flip through and toss around with her currents. The river would spin an endless tale at the bottom of the river and carry Marx and his sparrow out to the sea.

He scanned the other shore for any sign of the Pack; wary that their persistence would overturn his luck. The only omen of their presence was that same dense fog that shrouded the decaying wood from prying eyes. The old man wondered to himself whether the fog was to protect them from unwelcome intruders, confuse wandering prey, or disguise their deformity.

He wondered further if they were angry because they were tainted with the painful lesions of man or if the anger was the scar itself. Now he had given a ruined book to them in exchange for his life and passage.

In the manner that adults do, his grandfather once had a phrase that never truly made any sense until the reality was set before him.

"Giving is free, taking is what costs the most," was what he had said.

The Traveler had thought of himself as a pragmatic, logical person. However, the years of solitude had turned his thoughts to more intangible means, and he reflected on this phrase with a new appreciation. Over his many years, he had heard tales of man's corruption and seen through his travels the unforgiving nature of the world. In seeing the destitution of the pilgrim's village in the eastern plains, and now the echoing ravages of war, he now wondered if, at any point, the smoke had cleared and revealed a people tired of being unkind.

If the rage burned through all the hatred they had and left them with nothing else, would they not give, if given the chance? He finally understood this as the book had splashed into the depths of the river, taking with it his last, tangible link to what he knew. Stowed somewhere in his mind and consciousness, was a lurking guilt. The era he belonged to turned what should have been a thriving pack of creatures, with the grace of hares and the fierceness of wolves, into walking carcasses filled with rot and agony. It was not so much that he was giving them the useless book, but that he was relinquishing the part of himself that still could give and be glad to give. To him, it seemed a paltry favor, and served to do nothing other than ease only his discomfort, but it was all he had to give, and had to do. It was with that that he turned his back and walked back toward the woods beyond.

This thicket was less dense and malicious and busier with its own growth. It felt busy, and thrived with a chaos that alleviated the old man's loneliness. In a way that reminded him of his home on the mountain, the old man felt a peaceful manner of invisibility among the growing plants and chirping birds. As if he was merely visiting and mingling with the organisms that made up the atmosphere. The walking was easier with his lightened burden, and he was given permission to shorten his stride and allow his eyes to wander about his setting to admire a forest in its prime. There was plentiful light and the sun was warm enough for him to take some enjoyment from the day, but he knew he would need to restock if he was to keep starvation at bay.

Throughout his more pleasant walk, every once and a while a familiar leaf or root would catch his eye, and he would dig it up to reveal a wild vegetable. His mood lightened each time as he was able to make steady progress and be safe in the knowledge that he would eat again. Mile after mile, his pack and various sacks were growing heavier. His path forward led to more bounty and he was reminded that not everywhere he was going was filled with death and decay. In a stark contrast to the wood and plains behind him, new life was emerging busily seemed refreshingly unbothered by his heavy footfalls.

As each morning greeted him with warmer weather and gentle sunshine, he began to feel the tension in his shoulders loosen, and he slept deeper and sometimes allowed the fire to go out so that he could watch bats catch moths by moonlight. As many solitary travelers before him, he was lulled into safety and security and dropped his watchful guard. Until one day, he woke to a dreaded shroud of fog once more.

When the Traveler stirred from his slumber by the dying fire that morning, he saw that the once cheerful woods had been cloaked once again in mist. Dread seeped into his bones once more, and he threw together his pack and buried the flames in silent panic. His eyes peeled the edges of his vision for any shelter that could withstand a hungry pack. He moved silently while craning his ears for the cries and yips of their whining jaws and, when he heard the snapping of teeth and snarling surrounding him again, turned his eyes upward to look for a tree to climb out of sheer desperation. An old oak stood proudly above the fog and was sprouting new branches low enough for the old man to grasp at. He hoisted himself up branch by branch until he came to a thick enough limb to balance, skinning his forearms on the rough bark.

He ignored the sting and sat nervously waiting for them to circle. All there was were the sounds they made, he didn't see them. They howled to each other in their hunt and snapped at wherever they could find prey. A crunch betrayed a deer nearby, and its fate was sealed. The Pack descended and began their ragged chase of the unfortunate animal. Despite their malformation, these beasts were still hunters of considerable size and had no shortness of fang and frenzy.

The noises of their prey's death and their voracious feasting made his stomach churn as he slipped down from the tree and hustled away from the feeding frenzy. A week went by like this, the Pack hot on his heels and the fog always catching up with him. Each evasion was aided by luck and his increasing paranoia. Shelter was plentiful here, and his years of experience had honed him into a survivalist of considerable skills, despite his ailing constitution.

His luck held until he woke one morning to find the land clean of the fog, and his pursuers nowhere to be seen. The image of the land was crisp; not even a cloud in sight. The sky opened clear and blue above him. The Traveler looked around himself pensively, as if the ground might erupt in the familiar omen once again. It wasn't until his journey entered mid-morning that he felt at-ease and permitted himself a long sigh of relief. He had made it, and the Pack had turned its interest to other things. A break in the trees revealed open fields ahead; his surrounding of ready shelter was ending, and he would be open to new, unknown threats once more.

Worry burdened his thoughts as he exited the protective enclave of branches and bramble. These worries evaporated when he emerged into the meadow and took survey over the next chapter of his journey. His eyes traveled across the skyline and landed on buildings and other remnants of human life. A scattering of farmhouses with their big red barns across the yards. These fields were once pastures in which cattle would drift lazily about their days grazing and crooning at passersby.

He remembered cows; he was actually rather fond of them. He liked the way they wiggled their ears in glee when given treats or an attentive scratch at the chin. Once, when he was small, his grandparents had visited a farm with him in tow, and he got to see these gentle giants. His favorite was a ginger-spotted calf with white eyelashes and a pink nose. It had greedily plucked the sweet he offered from his palm and left a sticky thread of saliva. After it was finished grinding the sugar into dust, the calf nudged his hands for more, the spindly legs no more than propping up its clumsy little body.

It hadn't quite gained the robustness of adulthood. The now older man wondered if any of the cattle survived this long without their human guardians. His question was quickly answered when he came across a few of these animals. Happily strolling along the mossy green pastures, no longer constricted by the fences that lay in splinters along overgrown dirt paths, was a small herd with a few calves guarded by their mothers.

He was smarter than trying to approach, especially if there was a bull nearby. So, he passed them by slowly and carefully but met their eyes when they looked after him cautiously. The hours passed in relative peace as he weaved in between the farmhouses until he found one that he liked enough to camp out for the night with.

The House

He covered more ground that day now, that he wasn't stopping every hour to hide up a tree or bury himself in thickets. A broken road wound through the sleepy town, and he found himself grateful for the lack of roots and rabbit holes to avoid. He made camp on the outskirts of one of the larger towns, within a small cabin at the very edge. His journey had given him a wariness of the ruins of humanity and he hoped to avoid them in his walk's progression. His shelter sat next to a dilapidated main road leading north. It was still rundown and sad-looking but, to the man who had spent the last few weeks hiding in trees and swimming in rivers, it was a palace.

The old man was tired, no matter the pace, being pursued by something fatigues not just the soles of your feet, but the soul as well. He walked around the old house to survey its condition. It was a dark, oxidized yellow with black window shutters. It had two stories, and around the back, he found a large pile of firewood dry as bone and perfect for his use. There wasn't an intact window in the entire facade, but he saw no holes big enough for anything larger than a dormouse.

When his inspection was done, he concluded that at least the outside looked firm enough to keep out the wind and Pack if they dared to follow him again this far into old human territory. No sooner had he crossed the threshold into the house that his burdens slipped from his shoulders and fell to his feet. He swayed from the sudden imbalance and placed his hand to the peeling wall to steady himself. The house was silent, dormant. He left his pack by the door and went about the house unburdened.

First was the living room, with a small fireplace and a black rocking chair, so covered with dust that it looked to have fur, in the corner. The interior smelled like moss and old wood, *not unlike a book*, thought the old man. He went up the carpeted stairs and found that there were a couple of bedrooms, and a bathroom still in fair condition, but the beds were filthy with mildew and therefore ruined. *Pity*, he would have liked to sleep in a proper bed. Seeing the sun going down, the old man set about making his bed on the bottom floor.

The fireplace was stacked with wood and the hearth was sparked to life, and filled the walls with dancing light and radiant warmth. The house seemed to relax with its new tenant, and provided insulation and comfort that was sorely needed. He laid out his fur bed next to the hearth and crawled into its embrace *for just a moment*, he told himself. Normally, he would use his days of rest to hunt and forage and wash the filth itching his skin. There would still be much to do, but this time, the weariness caught up to him, and he slept.

While he slept, he dreamed more of the place that he was going to, a respite for him at his most tired and defeated. As he was coming to realize, the closer he came to his destination, the more vivid and real the recollection became, so the edges of this dream were not blurred and muddled. It was then that he understood the dusky dawn light that eternally permeated his dreams, casting its violet-gray hue upon everything, was the time he was last there. He remembered now, in the cerebral numbness that comes with dreams, he felt himself, as a child, being roused from his bed. Long gray hair tickled his face and the smell of lavender and oil wafted over him.

Grandmother was usually so composed and tidy, but the urgency in her voice spoke to her rush. Her strained whispers spoke of adventure and new promises. But now, with new clarity, he saw through her sweet lies and understood the fear in her eyes. As if he were no heavier than a doll, he was scooped into a protective embrace and wicked away into the night. He remembered the car and being nestled in-between parcels and bundles of belongings. His pajamas were still soft and warm on his skin, but, in wiggling his toes, he knew that his boots had been hurriedly pushed onto his feet; the wrong foot on the other. his young eyes, blurry with sleep, watched the sunrise beyond the cliffs as he was spirited away from that sweet house with the salty smell.

With the long journey, they would leave behind most of what they had brought and only carry what they could on their backs. The shrill song of sirens echoed in the distance behind them, and far away he could hear percussive landfalls and see the afterglow of fires that rained from above. He remembered that his grandmother never released his hand from her desperate grasp that night. Her smell of lavender soothed him when the terrifying sounds of war wrested him away from the comfort of sleep until he drifted back to fitful rest. She lured him forward every step of the way with promises of a special place, and someone waiting for him on the other side of the mountains.

A ray of warm sun peeked through the broken window to land in the Traveler's eyes, waking him from his dream. He rose slowly, not wanting to relinquish the reverie. His dreams always left him feeling wistful of his walk through life, and unsure of whether to be spiteful or grateful for the oath that brought him there. However, the wisdom and insight that only comes with age illuminated why this peaceful, old couple had risked everything to bring a child, not just away from calamity, but across the world. His sigh rattled his bones as he remembered.

His parents had lived across the mountains and likely quite some distance beyond. His whole exodus was to reach a home that he would never see again, he had gone the wrong way. He fell back into the embrace of his bed and let the realization crush him slowly. Somewhere along the journey, he had lost his way and his guides, his trail back had only brought him further away from the place that his grandparents spent the rest of their lives crossing to. He felt almost guilty as if he had undone their hard work and sacrifice. His parents had died or vanished long ago, and they would never see their son again. He wondered if they watched for him, carried over a continent, raised in the wild. The Traveler wondered what they might have thought of him on that mountaintop, with his peaceful, invisible existence, and what they would make of him now; journeying in search of home only to stray further away from them. He drifted in and out of a sad stupor and hopeless slumber; escaping these thoughts that now chased him.

He did not rise until about midday, until golden rays of light cascaded down from the zenith to peek through the windows of the desolate house fell on the eyes of the sleeper and woke him. The old man decided to explore the home a bit closer, perhaps he could find some supplies that he could not gain from the outside. He began upstairs in the larger bedroom and found that the dresser was fairly intact; the clothing inside was still dry and devoid of holes, albeit smelled of dust and darkness. The old man was pleased at the prospect of some fresh clothes; the clothing he had with him were threadbare and had the stench of travel on them. From the dresser, he pulled a shirt, trousers, and even a pair of socks. The material was thick and soft, but with the stink that time had given them, he decided to wash them before he wore them the first time.

While the newly laundered clothing was hanging on a makeshift clothesline in the yard, the Traveler saw fit to give himself a bath as well. There was a bathroom with a bathtub upstairs, but the plumbing likely hadn't worked for decades, so he hoisted bucket after bucket of hot water up the stairs until there was enough to sit in. By the time he lowered himself into the tub, the water had gone lukewarm, but it was miles better than the icy river, or not being clean at all. He had found some old soap in the cabinet that smelled like wood and some powerful musk he didn't recognize. It felt slippery on his skin, and he didn't like the pungent scent, but he was happy to be clean.

Newly refreshed, clean, and dressed in a fair quality shirt and sweater, the Traveler found that he felt much better than he did the day before. He looked at himself in the mirror of the bedroom to see himself clearly for the first time in decades. He took himself in with a dry humor that comes when one sees their own aging flesh. His gray hair was white now, the journey had aged him quickly and without mercy. He had lost weight and whatever muscle he had maintained was now sinewy and emaciated. His back hunched and his face was etched with the cruelty of time. The clothes didn't fit as well as he had hoped, the fabric hanging off his rugged frame.

Time had taken from him the stocky strength that he once had as a youth. He held out his hands and saw the bony wrists tremor slightly. His knuckles were thick and crooked. The mirror before him betrayed a man at the end of his life, a finite amount of possibilities lay before him. His tire and ache displayed before him in every dreadful detail.

Confronting his own weakness and fragility was more than he cared to take on that morning, but still, he stared at himself all the same. When the old man finally looked away, he found that his determination to finish his quest was renewed with an added desire to deny fate its conquest.

The rest of that warm golden day was spent in the busy preparation for another crossing. The lands ahead would be plentiful and open, but he was venturing into territory scarred by war and human desperation, and wasn't in the mood for surprises. Movement in the new clothes was different; the new fabric brushed against his skin in a new direction; the threads were rough and thick, but they would keep the wind from chapping his thinning skin. The feeling that the old soap left on his skin was definitely unpleasant, there was a layer of musky grease that he couldn't scrub away. Either way, he would have to get used to it, the appearance of fresh clothes and a bath was a blessing that he should be grateful for.

Before his wash, the old man had strung up all his mats and blankets to air out in the spring breeze. When he took them down, they smelled of the coming summer; the mustiness and river stench carried away. He continued with his day on a foraging trip into the woods. There were plenty of berry brambles and wild mushrooms to be had, and if he followed the wild herds of cattle they led him to edible grasses and leaves. While he was walking back, he looked back to the forest to see the fog again creeping out from the slender trunks.

This made him nervous, and he cut short what should have been a leisurely day. His head ducked behind him maniacally as he trudged away to see how much distance it crept. It crept closer each time he looked, but at a slower pace than usual as if the Pack within weren't pursuing but merely exploring their new home.

He arrived back at the house and bundled everything together to take refuge in the upstairs master bedroom. *Better to have only one entrance to watch than several*, he thought. Night fell over the faded walls and the sounds of the Pack echoed over the empty meadows. He barricaded the door and kept watch through the open window. The mist had now surrounded the homestead as the Pack sniffed at the threshold.

As he feared, the creatures ventured through the broken door and detected the remnants of his stay. Scratching thumps alerted his ears to their long claws scraping clumsily up the staircase. They stopped there as he had also possessed the forethought to bar the landing with a broken bedframe, behaving as bars to their advance. They wouldn't be able to pass through the forest of splinters and exposed nails.

He strained his ears to the howls of their discontent, but they left all the same. He watched three of them limp away into the cool darkness, taking their shroud with them. He wondered why their numbers were dwindling so quickly, and just how many there were to start with. Only after he was sure of their departure that he was at ease enough to relinquish consciousness to sleep.

The next morning was clear and filled with the sounds of birdsongs and merry chittering of squirrels. Once again, he had evaded the ancient ghosts that served as wardens here. He didn't loiter around and packed his things in a hurry to take advantage of the protective light of day. He left his useless, hole-ridden clothing folded neatly in the dresser drawer he had taken his new vestments from. Despite the emptiness of the place, the house separated him from the wild animals he journeyed past, and wanted to hang on to any sense of civility that he had left. The endless blue sky greeted him gladly as he emerged from the shelter to encounter the wild open once more.

After a few hours of early morning hiking, the lush rolling green landscape worked its magic and spelled a calmness on the old man. The fear and paranoia of being followed melted away like frost, and he was free to roam the countryside and take in the serenity that surrounded him. A cool wind whistled through the grasses and almost sang in a high-pitched whistle. The walk was easy, and he covered ground quickly, the salty scent guiding him home. Occasionally, he would come across a familiar landmark, a dead tree or a lone building.

They still peppered the land with splashes of red, brown, or more yellow paint. Each night he camped in a different house, observing how other people had lived their lives before the calamity, and the evidence of their flight. Much of the homes were left untouched as the inhabitants fled as quietly and lightly as they could in the dead of night. The panic had quickly arranged their priorities into anything that wasn't easily strapped to their backs was dead weight. He walked through their halls, looked at the books they had on their shelves, and saw the toys their children left behind.

He remembered painfully the fate that followed the survivors. People began to disappear into thin air, almost as if they were broken up along the horizon and swept away by the breeze. Stories whispered around shared tents and fires between whoever remained that they just gave up, that their troubles ate at them until there was nothing left. That must have been the case since there was no shortage of misery in this new world. The things they loved fell through their fingers like sand until all that remained was a fragile shell that the wind could blow away.

Wandering through the evidence of the lives people once lived formed a pit in the Traveler's stomach as he wondered what his own home would have looked like, if he had gone the opposite way.

The Cold Light

The summer reached its peak as he passed through an especially familiar sight. He had been traversing a bit of land when he noticed a shrinkage of the plant life. Rather than rejoicing in their dominion over the fertile soil, the stalks of grass seemed to pale and yellow from the root. The black asphalt roads weren't broken down and taken over by the earth but stood unyielding. He knew what this looked like, he'd seen this curious shyness where there was poisonous ruin nearby.

He was young at the time, but he still remembered what happened when no one was there to maintain the power-hungry cities of stone that rose high over the earth. They spewed a miasma into the air and leaked their venom into the dirt. When nature took back what was hers, she seemed to abandon these places and left them in their own filth. Though he rarely set eyes on these places, he never dared to venture in. Only the death they left in their wake, did he know their significance. The buildings stood small in the distance; with a few hours' travel, it would be in front of him in all of its grim glory.

The Traveler knew he could simply pass it by and put as much distance between him and the ruins as possible.

Curiosity, however, proved a persistent temptress, and it became so much that he could not turn away his steps. His boots took one stride after another, leading him toward the forest made by man. The sun had begun to retreat behind the hills when the old man arrived at his destination. This monument now stood before him in the fading light of summer sunset.

It was a massive collection of metal and brick, almost a mountain range in of itself. The spires of broken glass and metal towered above the terrain as a bleak, colorless mass. The road led deep into its center, like a giant tongue from the gaping maw of concrete. The smell in the air was metallic, like rust and blood. It felt stale and wrong.

Not only that, but for some reason the bulbs within the streetlights were still on. Their unnatural state was flickering and weak, but they still illuminated the road in a ghostly pale cascade. In his mind's eye, they looked like lost souls hanging their heads toward the ground, perhaps searching for themselves in the concrete. It was eerily silent; the dying light lent to the requiem.

The altered being of the city seemed to change time itself. The Traveler quelled his racing thoughts of worry and instincts to run and continued on. The bland, lifeless walls rose high in the sky to cut off his view of the earth around him. He felt encased here, as if in a giant coffin. They were not stone, even stone has unique and characteristic form. Nothing here preached anything other than obedience to the oppressive silence. Birds did not dare fly here.

Night fell on the walls and streets of the city. The old man continued his walk, illuminated by the ghostly streetlights and moon. She was at her fullest today, emanating the color of infectious death that strangely fit the atmosphere of the place. It was warm out tonight, but the light was cold. It illuminated everything in a joyless haze.

The Traveler stopped before the building in the heart of the city. His eyes were drawn upward to the vandalized exterior. A blurred vision from his past was now clear and present before him set in every dreadful detail.

There was a mural painted on the blank side of the building. He had a vague understanding of what it was, and what it meant for the calamity that displaced him; this. An image, whether it was the moon or something else bearing false witness to her, hovered high up on the wall. This was depicted high above the heads of surrounding spectators painted in brightly colored clothing and dark veils. Whether it was enraptured adoration, or the onset of terror painted on their faces he couldn't tell; it was strange how worship merges the two together. He recognized the drawings and tales from his travels east, when survivors gathered around fires and shared tales of survival, they pointed up to the sky, to the Cold Light. All he himself knew was that he feared it in the most primal sense. The acid in his stomach churned violently and formed a weight that seemed to pull him downward.

The heaviness dropped to his feet and held him frozen in place, in full view of the Cold Light that haunted his fever dreams and watched his world's destruction. Whenever the moon hung low and full, and the world was bathed in her glow, he thought of this image. The murals he was used to seeing were the hastily spilled, throwing of paint by someone in a hurry to escape, for it marked the pending calamity that unfolded in strange ways in strange places.

What was towering above him now was a carefully constructed work, but he knew all too well what it had meant for the inhabitants of the city.

On the very ground he was standing on, there had been a battle, perhaps one of the first. This patch of cool asphalt and concrete once soaked up the blood and tears of man. He had stumbled, once more, into a graveyard of human design. If he looked closely, he could see the shadows of brown bloodstains that rain refused to wash away, or that the strange time in this place neglected to fade. Either out of abhorrence for what happened here or for sorrow for lives lost, only the clouds and the Cold Light would know.

The old man waited quietly in the hallowed ground for a time when the command of his limbs was returned to him and the clicking of his steel-toed boots rang against the empty silence. He dared walk further among the buildings and structures; once the horror of what had happened here subsided, he was actually able to admire the bold architecture and design of the city. For all their many follies and missteps, humans were capable of such creativity. The meticulously crafted beauty of the carved stones and angular buildings came more readily to him now. He was able to see past the travesty of their extinction and marvel at what they left behind.

Monuments were skillfully carved from stone and marble in the form of angels and leaders walking proudly among the masses. There was even a park, now run dead and flattened, in the middle of this stone forest, people wanted green. That color of life was present even in places like this. The old man found a surprising comfort in that love of plants and life that he and the people of this city shared.

He didn't sleep that night, he only walked. The ghost lights and the altered state of the city chased sleep away. He passed through a suburban neighborhood that bore a faint resemblance to what he remembered. Green was timidly returning here, as if still hiding from the concrete and metal. The houses lay empty and overgrown with vines of ivy. If it wasn't so sad to see people's homes so distraught, then the old man would find it pleasing to see a merge of nature and manmade construction.

As he walked, the Traveler felt the familiar business in the air that replaced the haunt of the inner city. He felt more at ease here and relaxed enough to feel tired. He camped out there on the street with his fire built high and the sky above his head in the deepest blue-black. The streetlamps were still emitting their deadlights, hiding all but the brightest stars from view.

That night he dreamed of driving on these broken roads in a brown station wagon while watching the green foliage overtake the bleached ruins of civilization. Drowsy and calm, he entrusted himself to the unknown driver of that vehicle. The morning moisture in the air dispersed the light in a somber glow that seemed to stop all time and leave it hanging. Almost as if the earth kept it all entrapped in that moment, perhaps out of a hope of preserving something about this place.

He felt the same way; the gentle swaying and bumps of the car always lulled him to his most at ease. To allow the transfer of burdens to another and let yourself be carried along with them to safe harbor. That is the essence of trust, a feeling he hadn't known for quite some time.

That morning chased away the cold reverie of the previous night. The moment had passed and all that was left was the long road yet ahead. And he walked that path once more in slow resolution.

The Cliffs

The long days of summer drew on as the Traveler walked. Rolling hills of green became jagged with rocks until they spilled over into sheer cliffs overlooking the blue sea. *He was nearing his destination*, he thought to himself as he peered over the side into the churning waves below. The sea was a gray-blue with white, angry foam forming as wave after wave beat against the rocks and cliffside. The depth of the water was hypnotizing and strange.

It fed a secret curiosity in the Traveler that begged the question as to what manner of creatures lurked darkly under the surface. The behavior of the ocean changed often, not just with the weather but the light as well. Sunlight pierced the gray and revealed gem-like hues of teal and emerald within the azure element. Stormy skies and the indigo nights dyed them inky obsidian with the wind whistling over the water like a siren. To him, the ocean was a being in of itself; an ancient giant trapped in the deepest hole in the earth, unable to get free. All it could do was lash out with a foamy claw and slash at its stone prison walls.

The old man amused himself with this tale of a sentient ocean as he braced himself against the harsher winds coming in from the endless sea. It was something he used to do as a child, he recalled, to come up with mysterious tales to occupy the time. And in the absence of Marx's book, he enjoyed the fiction of it. But the curiosity remained in the back of his head, wondering silently what kind of beings swam along the sea floor.

He passed more houses that peppered the countryside; all of them broken down and faded versions of their former selves. He camped in a new one every night to linger within the walls of civilization once more. It made him feel more human, a sentiment that he realized had been missing these past decades. His journey of cowering by a warm fire and feasting on whatever he could find had made him feel more like a feral cat than a man.

The wide openness of the landscape seemed to let loose the clouds in the sky. Wisps of fluffy white vapor swept across the pale blue sky like dancers; the shadows over the land became an extension of their costumes. In addition to the beauty of it, they often provided temporary cover from the sun though only briefly. The Traveler found this walk easy with just the right amount of both. The fog was nowhere to be seen, so he felt safe once again and could enjoy his journey again.

Such peaceful weather made him feel energetic again, much like the beginning of his journey. He was able to take in the sights and sounds around him. His favorite color, green, surrounded him on all sides. Coupled with the enrapturing blue, his footfalls were lighter and more agile. His old bones still hurt, especially at the knees, but he was able to pay them less mind.

The prime weeks of summer were spent in this bliss. Walking leisurely through the fields and pastures, greeted by the birds that pecked at bugs on the backs of cattle and sheep. Each night he camped beneath the stars or in an abandoned house. He finally felt quiet and out of danger for the first time in the years of his travel. Even in the sanctuary of his mountain, he was under the watchful eye of the old deity making its patrol. Perhaps he was no longer trespassing, and was welcomed back to the cradle of man.

Steadily, as he made his way through the fair countryside of his origin, the greens of summer plenty were being replaced by the bright yellows and vermilions of autumn. The few trees that he came across were now brilliant palettes of color. A cold rain would tumble from the heavens and give the leaves a shine that made them glossy like blood. The old concrete road he followed soon became dusted with their hues.

It was when he arrived at a light blue signpost that he saw just how close he was. The lettering had all worn away with the peeling paint, but it was the presence of the sign itself that told him his location. He remembered this sign; he had last seen it on the car ride away. He was easily a few hours away from the last home he knew. The salt in the air was more pungent than ever from the sea beyond the cliff.

His pace quickened with anticipation. Before he realized it, he had broken out in an excited jog. His lungs burned from the excitement and the effort, but he pressed on until he came upon the first house.

It is one thing to begin a long journey and to see the road before you, and another to be in the midst of that adventure and feel stranded on all sides by the unfamiliar. But even more different, is the sentiment of having arrived at your destination.

To see the fruits of your labor and the rewards of your tears and blood. There is an apprehension as you reach out to close the remaining gap; you expect it to vanish before your very eyes and see that you have many yet more miles to go. The Traveler's destination lay before him, teasing him with its stillness. He had practically run here, but now he walked through the small village with a special slowness. Drinking in the sights of familiarity and belonging, he marched toward the edge of the cliff.

The Home

It was nearing sundown when he arrived within the village borders. His neighborhood was rundown and had been utterly desecrated by time and lay there drearily in the fading light. To him, however, it was immaculate. The white picket fences were peeled back to reveal rotting gray wood. The windows were smashed by rough winds and once finely manicured gardens were now shabby forests within themselves. He stopped and gazed tiredly down the street on both sides and took in everything.

Nature had claimed these houses and turned them feral. There was no stopped time for these homes, the world had not left them alone as it had the city. But he still knew them for what they once were, and the blurriness of his memory allowed the broken-down hovels to make themselves into what he had wanted to remember. *Three blocks from the left*, he reminded himself and turned the corner onto his street. His footsteps seemed to ring against the abandoned pavement.

He had learned how to ride a bike here with his grandfather's big hand on his back, pushing him forward, so he could feel the air. He remembered fondly pretending to forget how to pedal so that he could feel the rush of that push again. It was unlike anything he had ever felt before;

as a child, he thought he was flying faster than he could ever go by himself. He strained to remember the bike, not much coming to mind but knew the color was red like rust. Or it was supposed to be white and was just old. So, he resumed a slow pace down the boulevard, languidly casting his eyes this way and that, until he arrived at a pale-yellow house with a lavender garden.

He smelled the sharp freshness of the lavender before he even saw the house. Lavender was a tough plant and had survived through decades of seasons. The bushes framing the house had grown untamed and unabated; their blooms transformed into clouds of deep purple. They mirrored the sky in its dimming light. Almost a little patch of dusk all for himself.

Adding to the dreamy appearance of the cottage was a blue doorway with a rusted brass handle in an elegant oval shape, not unlike a shell. The old man reached out and cupped his hand around the rounded metal; it's cool surface peppered with a rough coating of rust. The cool metal felt nice against his skin, so solid and perfectly fitted. It turned slowly in his hands and with a quiet click, it swung open to welcome him home.

After he stepped into the foyer, the straps of his pack slumped from his shoulders, and his stave tumbled to the ground. He was a lonesome, wandering Traveler no more. His things landed with a thud that rang through the empty halls. The walls were a creamy white, he had forgotten that, the years of solitude and exposure to the wet ocean gales had tinted them ochre, but he remembered now. The curtains were yellowed too, and the furniture faded from the dark blue they had once been.

There was a basket of sewing supplies that lay abandoned in a basket by a coffee table. His steps caused the floorboards to creak as he ventured further in, the obnoxious noise resounding through the silence. There was a kitchen with blue plates caked in dust, still set neatly at the table awaiting supper. Everything was neat and tidy, albeit covered in dust and bleached by the sun. He moved onto the upstairs.

His grandparent's bedroom was painted a light green and slate, the bedspread the only thing that wasn't in its place. As if it was thrown off and never tucked back in. A footprint left by their quick flee. Their bathroom was just as neat, elegant glass bottles of perfume sat on a mirrored chest of drawers. He lifted each to his nose and breathed deep from the sweet elixirs. Compared to their long narrow shapes was the stout roundness of his grandfather's aftershave. He smelled that too, reacquainting himself with them as he liked envisioning them. He liked remembering them as if they were going to church on Sunday morning, put together and enjoying the day. His reverie was interrupted by him catching a glimpse of himself in the dirty mirror. His hair was still ashen, and the line of his face seemed to point down to the ground. His character was carved into his flesh now, no smile lines or signs of a merry life, only grim survival.

However accustomed he was to himself now, he felt that his face must feel strange to the home that protected him; it was used to a boy, not a broken old man. He put down the perfumes and aftershave and left the bathroom. The hall was dark when he emerged from the master bedroom. Just down the hall now, to his room, and the shadows followed him like kindly ghosts.

The door was open; a small green scarf was draped over the doorknob in the careless manner of a child. His grandmother had always hated that, the sloppy half-hazard discard of his clothing. A habit he had never gotten rid of until she had gone, and he grew from a child to a man. He leaned into the doorway, and there was his bed; the thing he had always woken from in his dreams, once he left this bed for the last time, he was never the same. Hovering above it were the cotton curtains that on fair nights would flap lazily in a seaside breeze.

The window was closed and the glass intact; no moisture had gotten into the room to soil the bed or wallpaper. Everything was just as he had left it, crumpled, messy, and all his linens in a pile. Just the way he liked it. There was something about seeing how small he used to be that exaggerated how old he had gotten. He towered over the toys and pajamas; the unkind years wore away any childlike softness and rendered him into a broken statue with protruding ribs and deep lines etched into his long face.

The old man was on his last legs, but he had endured and returned home at last. He let himself sink heavily onto the small mattress and curled up with his own sheets wrapped around him. They were so small that they didn't even fully cover his shoulders, but he found that he no longer cared. The warmth was leaving his body in a permanent, but not uncomfortable way, and he found that he needed no more blankets than what he had. He reached out and pried open the old window to let the chilly sea air in. It swung open and a draft blew in from beyond the cliffs.

There he slept, long and heavy in the bosom of his home recovered. It was not the place he was hoping to reach, nor was it where his elders had hoped to bring him, but it was his. Lulled by the salty, lavender-laden breeze blowing softly through the cotton curtains; their white now yellowed from time. A lost child had finally come home to rest and dwell quietly for the rest of his days in the fractured remains of peace and belonging.

There, in a soft bed too small for him, he dreamed. He dreamed of being pulled from his bed as a child and spirited away through the territory of deep scars left by humanity's plight. He dreamed of crossing a wide-open plain filled with the unseen terrors of an ancient dried-up sea. Of a small creature of sadness left there to wither away with the memories that defined her. He dreamed of seeing the mountains rise tall before him and venturing forward with his hands held on both sides, only to arrive alone at the top to stay for a lifetime.

There he saw again the towering king of the mysterious woods, a monument to the dawning age of a new nature. He dreamed bitterly of the destination that had cost lives and years to reach, only for him to turn back to where it all began. He dreamed of warm love and the thrill of adventure, the gifts that life, embodied in green, had given him. He dreamed of death, swathed in the color white, who had revoked those gifts and left him broken and cold in the heart of winter. Now, he found himself staring at the very edge of all things, beyond green, white, love, loss, and fear.

He stared deeply into the welcoming abyss of the deep, wild blue.